The Passion

of

Bronwyn

Martina Martyn

*For Aimee
With Love*

Dylan Publications

Dylan Publications

This paperback edition 2013

First published by Dylan Publications 2013

Martina Martin asserts the moral right to be identified as the author of this work

This novel is entirely a work of fiction. The characters, names and incidents portrayed in it are the work of the author's imagination. Any resemblance to real persons, living or dead, events or localities is entirely coincidental.

To Martin

&

All my Family

PROLOGUE

She was known to all her family as Aunt Wyn. She seemed incredibly old when I was a child. Her skin was like parchment, wrinkled but soft, and she wore small Dickensian spectacles. On her head she always wore a small hat and underneath it her hair was grey. She always wore it drawn back and pinned into a bun. I only ever saw her wearing a long black dress with a starched pinafore over the skirt. Under her skirt she always wore buttoned boots. She was very thin, quite tall and walked with a decided stoop and she was the kindest, gentlest person I knew. I used to visit her with my mother and it was like going through a time warp and turning the pages right back into the nineteenth century. The living room was smallish and she was always sitting right up close to the biggest coal fire you ever saw so the room was always very hot. She would sit upright, almost like she was holding court. She was also terribly deaf so we always had to shout to make ourselves heard. As a child my overwhelming impression was of intense heat and noise but I looked forward to going to visit her. We all presumed she was just a maiden aunt. I have since found out that she was my Great Grandmother.

CHAPTER ONE

Her story starts in the small Welsh coastal town of Penarth. Her name was Bronwyn Williams and she lived with her mother, Violet Williams and father Leonard Williams. She had a half-brother, Henry, brother, Robert and two sisters, Gwyneth and Elizabeth who were both younger than her. Henry's mother had died when he was very young but he had never accepted his stepmother and half-brother and sisters. He had turned into a nasty bully who treated his half siblings like slaves. He was older and bigger than them and attacked them whenever he thought he could get away with it. They were a poor family but because their father was a fisherman, they always had fish to eat. They grew vegetables in the tiny plot of land that the house stood on. It was a busy town so there was work for all of them on the docks, although they didn't earn very much money as they still had to attend the local school and could only work when the school day ended. Wyn was the best one at gutting the fish so she was given the best fish her father caught to gut in the shed at home. Every Sunday they all went to the local church as their mother and father were very religious.

After Church the children were free to do what they wanted. They would go down to the docks and watch the boats come in. There was a lot of coalmining done around the area and the coal was transported by boat. There was always a lot of shouting and men rushing about and Wyn, Elizabeth and Robert enjoyed watching all the activity. It was always a peaceful time for them because Henry would go off on his own. None of them knew what he was doing but at least it gave them a break from him. The bullying was getting much worse. He would hit and pinch them until they had bruises on their bodies but he was clever enough to only do it where nobody could see it. He had also started touching Wyn in places she shouldn't have been touched. She would tell him not to touch her but he would just laugh and say try and stop me then and she would try very hard but he was too strong for her.

One day Wyn came home to find her mother crying. She ran over to where her mother was sitting and asked her what was wrong. Her mother told her that Henry had been taken by the police and her father was very upset. It seemed that Henry had been caught stealing from the big house on the hill. There were three policemen upstairs searching Henry and Robert's room. Henry had a box of things he had collected over the years. There were different coloured stones and pebbles he had picked up off the beach so they knew it belonged to him. In there they found small bits of jewellery and silver ornaments. Henry was taken away and Wyn, Elizabeth and Robert hoped they would not see him for a long time.

Henry was found guilty of theft and was sent to Cardiff Prison for four years. He managed to avoid a longer sentence and transportation as he was only 14 years old and it was the first time he had been caught. He left court with his usual swagger pretending to everyone that time in prison didn't scare him. He especially didn't want his half-brother and sisters to know. He needed to know they were all scared of him, it made him feel he was a real man.

During this time life went on peacefully. They were still very poor but always seemed to have enough food to eat. Leonard missed Henry but started giving more attention to the other children. Life for all of them was tough but good. It was summer time and the weather was warm. Since the railway had come to Penarth there were always a lot of day trippers coming to the seaside. There had also been a lot of Hotels built and they loved just watching the holidaymakers coming and going. There always seemed to be something going on to watch.

They lived in a beautiful area, miles of countryside set with corn fields, pasture land, tall hedges and winding lanes. There was purple heather on the hills and gleaming in the distance, was the dark blue brilliance of the sea. During one of their walks in the hills after school they met a strange little boy with bare feet who was very dirty. His name was Bert and he lived with his granddad in a hut on the other side of the hill. He started meeting them whenever they went up the hill. They would explore the countryside and got very good at recognising the calls of the birds. After running around the hills all day they would visit Bert's granddad and he would give them a drink of milk from his own cow and tell them stories about his life when he was a small boy. He became a coal miner when he was about 14 years old. Life down the mines was very hard and after breathing in the coal dust for so many years, he had a cough that never stopped.

The next time they met up with Bert he told them he was leaving Penarth because his grandfather had died and he had to go and live in the city with an older cousin he had never met. He felt very sad about going and told them he would miss them very much. He had never lived in a city and didn't want to go. As he turned to go he gave Wyn a four leaf clover he had found.

'Keep this and you'll have good luck,' he told her and he started walking away. Wyn ran over to him with tears in her eyes and kissed him on the cheek.

'Bye,' she said, 'hope it will be alright in the city.'

As Bert got to the brow of the hill he turned and waved. That was the last time they saw him.

Then came the day that none of them were looking forward to, Henry came home. He was bigger and meaner and although his father was overjoyed to see him, the other children were not so happy. They knew their lives would no longer be happy and carefree. The beatings and abuse started again straight away. They tried to keep out of his way but in a small house it was not possible. They started staying away from home until they knew their parents would be there. Their mother would fuss over Henry giving him the best food because she said he had lost a lot of weight in prison and needed feeding up. She would ask the other children why they stayed away but never listened long enough to let them explain. They were so unhappy, Wyn more than any of them as she was the one Henry would pick on most. She tried to keep him away from her younger sister and brother and most of the time succeeded. It was getting much worse for her and she was very scared about how it would end. She couldn't tell anyone about the times Henry would trap her alone and touch her in her private places. He would fondle her budding breasts and put his hand up her skirt. She would feel a hard lump as he pressed himself against her. She was scared because she knew that what he was doing was wrong and she knew it was just a matter of time before something very bad happened. Sometimes she would go into the shed to start gutting the fish and he would be in there with the front of his trousers open. He would jump, stop whatever he was doing and smack her round the face for disturbing him.

It was a few weeks later when Wyn was woken up by footsteps coming along the rotten floorboards of the landing. She woke up her sleeping sisters Elizabeth and Gwyneth. Wyn told them to get down by the side of the bed as she knew he couldn't get to them there. They lay there shaking with fear but just as the footsteps got to their bedroom door, a voice came from downstairs.

'Who's moving around up there?' asked their father.

'It's just me,' Henry replied, 'I thought I heard something.'

'Well get back to bed,' their Father said.

The footsteps stopped and then went back slowly towards the boy's room. That was close Wyn thought; it's getting harder to stop him. She looked down at her sisters and told them that it was safe to get back into bed.

The next day Wyn was outside in the shed gutting the fish their father had been out catching when Henry walked in. He went up behind her and without saying a word he pulled her skirt up, unbuttoned himself and roughly pushed his already erect member inside her. Wyn felt a tearing pain and shouted, 'stop it, you're hurting me.' She screamed but he just said, 'stop screaming, there's no-one here to help you, they're all out working.' Wyn was very scared but still threatened to tell their father but Henry just started thrusting harder into her. He was breathing heavy and was moaning loudly. Wyn just gritted her teeth until he finished.

'If you tell Father,' he said, 'I'll just do it to Elizabeth, it's up to you.'

Wyn knew she couldn't let it happen to one of her sisters as she had always felt very protective of them. Henry just laughed, wiped himself on a rag and then walked out.

From then on whenever he could, he would force her to submit to him. It went on for a long time and she started feeling guilty because her body had started responding to him and she felt stirrings of pleasure when he pushed harder and harder into her.

One day she was out in the shed gutting the fish and, as usual Henry came up behind her and was just unbuttoning himself when her father, Leonard, walked into the shed.

'Henry!' he yelled, 'what are you doing you filthy bastard, get off your sister.'

He turned to Wyn and told her to run back to the house and go up to her bedroom.

'I'll come and see you shortly,' he told her.

Henry slowly re-buttoned himself and turned round and just smirked at his father. Leonard hit him with all the strength he could muster. Henry fell to the ground and sat there dazed with blood pouring from his nose. Leonard sat on a bench and looked at his son.

'How did you turn out to be so bad?' he asked. 'What am I going to do with you? You can't stay here with your sisters; you obviously can't keep your hands off them.

Henry just looked back at him and didn't reply. Leonard sighed, sat and thought for a while and then got up, locked Henry in the shed and went down to the dock. The previous night in the local Inn, he had been talking to the captain of a ship that was sailing to the West Indies the following day and the captain had mentioned that he was looking for crew. The ship was still there so Leonard asked to see the captain then told him all about Henry and how bad his behaviour had become.

'You said you needed crew,' Leonard said, 'will you take Henry? He's strong, fit and used to hard work. I don't want him to end up in prison again.

'Alright,' the captain agreed, 'I am desperate for crew.'

They both went back to the house to get him. Henry was still sitting in the same position in the shed.

'You are going with the captain,' Leonard told him.

'You're not to argue or make a fuss, it's either this or the police, I leave it up to you.'

Henry gave him an evil look but agreed to go. '

'Don't worry Leonard,' the captain said, 'you'll not be seeing him for a long time. What are you going to tell your wife?'

'I'll just say he's been thinking about going to sea for a long time and you made him a good offer,' Leonard told him.

With Henry gone, Leonard now knew he had to get Wyn away from Penarth before there was any chance of a scandal. The only person he could think of to help her was Father John. He knew a lot of people. Leonard walked down to the Church where Father John was in the vestry. He looked at Leonard and saw something was troubling him. He asked him if there was a problem and Leonard explained what had been happening and asked if John could help get Wyn away from Penarth. Father John told him that he did know of a family in London that might take her in.

'She would have to be willing to work very hard and it wouldn't be an easy life. It would be very strange for her at first.'

Leonard replied that she would be better off away from there. 'You never know,' he said, 'she might even like it.' Father John told him that he would make the arrangements. He said the train fare could come out of the poor fund and that he would let him know when she should go. Leonard thanked him and walked home with a heavy heart. Not only had he lost his eldest son but now his favourite daughter had to leave. How was he going to explain this to Violet without telling her the real reason why?

When he got home Wyn was lying on her bed staring at the ceiling. Leonard walked in and told her that Henry had gone and wouldn't ever touch her again. He also told her he had been speaking to Father John and they had decided that the best thing for her to do was get away in case anyone ever found out what had happened.

'Where am I going?' she cried, 'I don't want to leave my family. I want to stay here. Please don't make me go. I tried to stop him but he said he would do it to Elizabeth if I told you.' Leonard hugged her, 'I know it wasn't your fault, he told her, 'you did right protecting your sister but it will be better for you if you leave. This could be a chance for you. You won't have to gut fish for the rest of your life.'

He left Wyn and went downstairs. His wife Violet was sitting darning. She looked up as he walked in and could see by his face something bad had happened.

'What's wrong?' she asked. He told her that Henry had

decided to join a ship going to the West Indies. Violet looked at him in shock.

'What's happened?' she asked, 'when will he be going?' Henry told her that the ship had already sailed.

'It was a last minute decision. He was very happy the captain would take him. It's a hard life but it's what he wanted.' Leonard then told her the hardest bit, 'Father John has told me that he can arrange a better life for Wyn as well. He knows of a family in London who is looking for a scullery maid.' Violet looked at him, 'what's going on?' she asked. 'Henry gone, now Wyn going. I'm not stupid, what's been happening?'

'Nothing's going on,' Leonard replied, 'it's just that these things are happening at the same time. Don't you want better lives for them both? Maybe Father John can sort something out for Gwyneth and Elizabeth when they are old enough.'

Violet gave him a strange look but said, 'of course I want a better life for them but I'll miss them so.'

Two weeks later Wyn found herself at Penarth station with Leonard and Father John. Her mother wasn't there because she just couldn't face seeing her eldest daughter leave. They had said their goodbyes earlier and Violet had now taken to her bed totally devastated at the loss of her eldest daughter. Father John had found Wyn a place in a large house in Chester Square, Belgravia. The house belonged to Charles and Hester Brompton who had made their money from a sugar plantation in Jamaica. Wyn would be working as a scullery maid. It wouldn't be an easy life for her but at least she wouldn't have to put up with Henry anymore. Wyn was very scared and unhappy and didn't want to leave the only place she had ever known.

The train was hot, stuffy and smelly It was the first time Wyn had ever been on a train and at first she didn't like it, but as she got used to the motion, she started to enjoy it and was fascinated watching the different scenery going past the windows. She had only ever known the sea and hills but now she was seeing larger towns. The train journey went past very fast and they were soon coming into Paddington Station. It was very noisy with people running around and shouting and she saw a few ladies who had very painted faces and bright clothes. She had never seen ladies like that before. She nearly asked Father John who they were but something in his face stopped her. They were met by the Second Footman of the house. His name was William Taylor and he escorted them to the waiting carriage. William was only 15 and had been working in the house for two years. He looked at Wyn with a worried expression and commented, 'you're a skinny little thing, I don't think you're going to be strong enough to be a scullery maid.'
'She's stronger than she looks,' Father John told him. Wyn said nothing; she was too terrified by all the strange noises and smells. The streets were full of shouting people and there was rubbish everywhere. After they had been travelling for about an hour they arrived at the house. William took them down the basement steps and through the kitchen door. They went into the kitchen where the cook, Mrs Davis was waiting.
'Well, what have we got here,' she asked.
'This is the new scullery maid, Bronwyn Williams,' he

told her.

'Bit skinny for the job,' she said, 'but I'm sure we can get her working.' She turned to Father John and asked him if he could wait for a minute as the housekeeper wanted to see him. She turned to William and asked him to go and tell Mrs Danvers that they were there.

It was about ten minutes later that Emily Danvers, the Housekeeper, came through the door. She was Father John's sister and a kind and compassionate woman.

'Hello John,' she said, 'is this the waif you have been writing to me about? Are you sure she will be able to fulfil her duties? She's a bit young.'

Father John smiled and replied, 'Wyn's spent most of her life so far gutting fish so she's stronger than she looks. I just had to get her away,' he said, 'she deserves a chance of a new life.'

Emily turned to Wyn and told her that it wouldn't be an easy life. Wyn looked at her and replied, 'I don't care, I don't ever want to go home. I never want to see my parents again. They sent me away. I'll work hard I promise.'

Emily turned to Mrs Davis and said, 'Wyn is now in your care and you are to treat her kindly.' She then turned to Wyn and told her that she was in good hands and that she would be looked after. Emily smiled at Wyn and left the kitchen. Wyn jumped when Mrs Davis suddenly shouted, 'Betty come here I need you.'

Betty, the kitchen maid appeared. She was an untidy, very tall and slim redhead with a mass of freckles on her face. 'What you shouting me for?' she asked.

'Less of the cheek,' Mrs Davis replied. 'This is Wyn, the

new scullery maid; show her up to your room. She will be sharing with you.'

Betty looked at Wyn and replied, 'that room isn't big enough to swing a cat in, how are we both going to sleep in there?'

'Stop your moaning,' said Mrs Davis, 'at least it will be warmer with two of you. Just get yourselves up there and show Wyn where the ablutions are too.'

The servants in this house were very lucky as Mr & Mrs Brompton believed in looking after their servants well and there was a water closet on the servants floor, although they still had to carry water for washing and for the old tin bath they had to bathe in front of the fire in their room. Betty took Wyn up to the top of the house where Wyn walked into the smallest bedroom she had ever seen. There was only one bed, a wardrobe and a vanity unit to house the washing bowl and jug, in the room. The sheets were thin and threadbare but very clean.

'I suppose Mrs Davis was right,' said Betty, 'it will at least be warmer with the two of us in the bed. I just hope you don't snore.'

Wyn just stood in the doorway not saying anything. The events of the last few days were beginning to catch up with her and she had gone into a state of shock. What's happening to me, she thought how did I end up here? Betty could see how she was feeling so got hold of her arm and pulled her into the room, laid her down on the bed and told her to sleep for a while as she wasn't going to start work until the following day.

Betty went back to the room a couple of hours later to

find Wyn awake and looking more alert. 'Come with me,' she told her, 'I'm to take you to Mrs Danvers because the mistress wants to see you.'

Betty took Wyn down to the kitchen where Mrs Danvers was waiting to take Wyn up to the drawing room to see Mrs Brompton. When they walked into the room Wyn saw an attractive woman with long blond hair done up in a bun. She was very slim and was wearing a fashionable day dress. She looked at Wyn and said to Mrs Danvers, 'she is only a child, how is she going to be able to do the work of a scullery maid?'

'I'm told she is stronger than she looks,' replied Mrs Danvers, 'she is used to hard work.' 'Alright,' replied Mrs Brompton, 'I'll leave her in your care.' Then she turned to Wyn and said, 'if you work hard and do as you are told you will be alright here. Go along now and do as Mrs Davis tells you.'

CHAPTER TWO

Wyn settled into the life of the house. It was hard work in the kitchen. She had to get up at six o'clock, wash and dress and make sure her hair was tied neatly back beneath her cap. Her bed had to be made properly and she had to be downstairs at work within half an hour of waking to start her first task of the day which was to bring the kitchen range up to a good heat to boil the water for early morning tea for the other servants. She then had to clean the kitchen, pantries and scullery. Her duties were physically demanding and never stopped during the day. Her last tasks before the servant's supper were cleaning the kitchen floor, stoves, sinks, pots and dishes. She always felt very tired but wasn't unhappy. Her life had more peace in it because there was no worry about Henry hurting her or her sisters. Wyn liked the mornings best when she had to be dressed in a clean apron for morning prayers in the Main Hall, as this was the only time she ever went upstairs. She looked forward to this as it gave her a chance to see William who had become a good friend since she had arrived. She did manage to have a break after lunch for an hour. She and William would stand outside the back door and talk and laugh. He made her life surprisingly happy. Her duties would then carry on until the servant's supper at half past nine when she was free until she had to go to bed.

Wyn had been working in the house for three years and it was getting harder to think about how her life had been in Wales. She and William had become closer and they spent as much time together as possible. One night, as they were standing outside looking up at the stars he looked intensely at her and said, 'I really want to kiss you.'

'Oh, I couldn't,' she exclaimed, 'it wouldn't be right.'
'No-one can see,' he said, grabbing her hand as she passed in front of him to retreat back into the kitchen. He pulled her into his arms, put his hand under her chin and lifted her face to look at him. He gazed down into her eyes and she couldn't resist him any longer. As he bent his head down, she let her lips brush gently against his. She'd never been kissed before and didn't to know what to expect. Kissing William felt so good. His lips were soft yet demanding, and his tongue gently tickled her lips. She opened her mouth, allowing him to deepen the kiss as he pulled her closer to him. He let his hands wander, one hand taking out her hairpins, allowing the brown locks to tumble down her shoulders, while his other arm wrapped itself around her slender waist pulling her closer. She shivered as the kiss went on, frissons of pleasure rippling through her body. Oh, it was wrong to kiss him, but it felt so right. William suddenly pushed her off his lap as Betty came out of the kitchen door. Wyn sighed in disappointment as she hadn't wanted it to end. Betty looked at them both and shook her head.
'You know if Mrs Davis finds out you'll be in big trouble,' she told them, 'servants are not allowed to do that sort of thing.'
'I don't see why not,' William said, 'we are people with feelings too.'
'Just be very careful,' Betty warned them.
That night in bed Wyn turned to Betty and asked her if she had ever been in love. Betty looked at her and replied, 'no I haven't and I don't want to be. It always leads to trouble mainly for the woman. Don't get carried away and let a

man touch your body anywhere. If he does, it could get you into deep trouble and don't believe he will marry you either. That's how they get you. They promise marriage but it's never true.'

'But I really like William,' Wyn sighed, 'he makes me feel all tingly and funny.'

'Oh go to sleep, I'm so tired,' replied Betty. 'It's another busy day tomorrow. The family have guests coming for the house party and we'll be very busy in the kitchen. Mrs Davis will be shouting and hollering. She'll be after you too.'

The next evening there were several carriages drawing up outside the front door at regular intervals. The door was opened by William who was dressed in his finest uniform of dress coat and pumps. Mr Carter, the butler, then took their hats and coats and conducted them to the drawing room where Mr & Mrs Brompton were waiting to receive them. Mr Carter then served them with a glass of sherry before they were shown to their rooms. The guests had brought their own maids and valets with them and they were let in the kitchen door by Betty. Mrs Danvers then led them up to the first floor where they were shown to their masters and mistresses rooms. The servants also had a small room next to them.

Wyn could hear the giggling of the women and the loud voices of the men from her vantage point on the stairs to the kitchen. She and Betty had been busy from first light helping Mrs Davis in the kitchen and were now sitting exhausted with a cup of tea.

'I'm done in,' Betty exclaimed. 'I'm so glad I'm finished until after dinner.'

'Yes but isn't it exciting?' commented Wyn, 'I love seeing all the lovely clothes and jewellery the ladies are wearing and doesn't Mrs Brompton look beautiful?' she asked Betty.

'Yes,' Betty replied, 'but did you see the looks Mr Charles was giving that tall lady in the red satin? Her husband certainly noticed. Now that could make it exciting.'

The gong sounded for dinner at 8.00 pm precisely. All the guests then went into the dining room led by Charles Brompton and the most important female guest, Lady Hetty Porchester who was the lady in red satin that Wyn and Betty had noticed Mr Charles looking at earlier. Hester Brompton brought up the rear with Sir John Porchester who wasn't taking his eyes off Charles or his wife. After dinner the Ladies withdrew into the drawing room for coffee for a short time while the men had their port. Then the real entertainment of the night started. They were all playing cards. It was one of their favourite pastimes and was taken very seriously. Charles Brompton loved to play Baccarat but unfortunately for him, was not very good at it. That night he lost a lot of money.

Wyn and Betty had been told to help with the clearing of the table and the washing up of the dishes. The guests had already left the table so they went into the dining room to find a total mess. Some of the guests had got a little over excited and had started throwing food at each other.

'That's all we need at this time of night,' said Betty, 'it's going to take us hours to sort this lot out.'

'Come on,' Wyn said, 'the sooner we start, the sooner we finish. Look at these plates, don't you think they're lovely?' The whole dinner service was made of delicate china with a gold stripe around the rim and flowers in the middle.

'Right at this moment, I don't care what the plates look like, I just want to get out of here,' grumbled Betty. Two hours later they had finished and were sitting in the kitchen relaxing with a cup of tea before they went to bed. Mrs Davis was sitting in a chair dozing in front of the fire when the door opened and William walked in.

'You should hear the noise coming from the drawing room. I think someone has lost a lot of money at cards. There's a lot of shouting that someone had been cheating,' he said. 'I reckon you should get to bed. There's going to be trouble tonight and I don't think you girls should be downstairs when it starts.'

Sure enough, just after Wyn and Betty went to bed they heard a lot of doors banging and men shouting at each other. They could also hear the quiet voice of Hester Brompton trying to calm things down. Eventually they heard footsteps heading up the stairs as everyone retired for the night. The house went quiet.

'That sounded like an interesting party,' Wyn remarked, 'I hope everything is alright now.' She was just dropping off to sleep when she heard a scream coming from one of the bedrooms. The house was suddenly full of noise with people running along the corridors. 'What do you think has happened Wyn?' asked Betty.

'I don't know, Wyn replied. 'Try and ignore it and get some sleep, it's nearly time to get up already and I'm still tired. It's nothing to do with us.'

The next morning they went down to the kitchen to start work to find Mrs Davis already in the kitchen. 'Sit down she told them. Did you hear all the noise last night?' They both nodded.

'It was because Mr Brompton accused Mr Porchester of cheating at cards and in return Mr Porchester accused Mr Charles of trying to seduce his wife,' she informed them.

'After everyone went to bed Mr Porchester sneaked into Mr Charles's room and tried to strangle him. Fortunately for Mr Charles, Mrs Brompton was in the room with him. She was the one who screamed.'

'Where are they all now?' asked Wyn.

Mrs Davis replied that the house party had ended early and everyone would be leaving shortly.

'The Porchesters have already gone,' she said. 'No-one wants to involve the police.

CHAPTER THREE

Although Charles Brompton owned a very large sugar plantation in Jamaica that gave him a very respectable living, he had lost a lot of money recently and after the events of the previous night Hester had decided that the only way to save him and the London house was by taking him to the country straight away. There had been too many witnesses to what had gone on and she was very concerned that they would be ostracised by London Society. She did not want to lose the house or anymore of the servants. Times were hard for below stairs staff and she didn't want them homeless without a job because of her husband's gambling habit. She summoned Mrs Danvers and told her to get the household ready to leave the next day.

The next morning was chaos with staff running all over the house. Mrs Danvers was shouting orders at all the housemaids and Mr Carter was shouting instructions to all the footmen. It was relatively calm in the kitchen. Mrs Davis was packing a few items she felt they would need that wouldn't already be in the country house. Betty and Wyn were packed and ready to go. They were just sitting having a last cup of tea waiting to leave.

'Alright,' said Mrs Davis, 'get yourselves upstairs, the coach is here to take you to the station.'

Betty and Wyn were feeling really excited to be going. William had told them they would have a lot more spare time there. They were piled in the coach with all the luggage. 'Blimey,' exclaimed Betty, 'look at all this stuff. How long are we going for?'

They were soon at the station. It was very busy with people shouting and rushing around. William was there to greet them and showed them into their compartment in the train. As they were servants they obviously didn't travel first class but Mr Charles had made sure they had their own carriage.

'We'll be there in about two or three hours,' said William, 'so make yourselves comfortable. Mrs Davis will be along shortly with food for the journey.'

'Which carriage are you in?' asked Wyn.

'I'm with the other footmen two carriages down,' replied William. 'See you when we get there.'

Mrs Davis appeared with packed lunches for them just as the train started to move.

'I'm in here with you two,' she said, 'so behave yourselves.'

The two girls looked out of the window at the scenery flashing past. It was hard to see much at times because of all the steam. Betty marvelled at the countryside she was seeing. She was a London girl and had never been outside the city before. The time went past very fast and they were soon coming into the station. They were met by a groom from the house. His name was Frank Cooper and he looked very happy and friendly. He had a ruddy red face with hair nearly the same colour. He was very thin but the girls could see he was quite muscular with sun darkened skin. He came up to them whistling and gave them a smile.

'Your carriage awaits,' he told them, 'don't worry the luggage will be picked up separately, you just come with me.' Wyn. Betty & Mrs Davis followed him to where there was a horse and trap waiting for them. They all clambered in but Frank had to help Mrs Davis up.

'Where are we?' asked Wyn.

'We're near the village of Ripplesdown,' replied Frank. 'The house is just the other side of the village, it won't be long now.'

It was late in the afternoon when they finally went down a deep narrow lane and saw the house shimmering in the late afternoon sunlight. It was a grey-stone mansion with large chimneys and a pond with a small fountain at the front. It was surrounded by fields and there was a stream running through the nearest one. There were cows in the field and ducks swimming in the stream. Wyn was captivated by the sights around her and for the first time started feeling slightly homesick. Frank drove the trap round to the back of the house and they all jumped down. They were met at the back door by Mrs Danvers. She told them to go into the kitchen and wait until she was ready to show them their rooms. When Mrs Danvers was ready, she took Wyn and Betty on a mini tour of the house. They looked inside a couple of rooms opened mouthed. They had never seen anything like this before. The house in London was opulent but this was much, much better. They walked into the drawing room of the house which was decorated with rich tapestries. The wall coverings were made of leather and Mrs Danvers told them they had been there since 1862. There were Dutch paintings in the Dining Room and the library had over 5,000 books and was used by the family to gather in before and after lunch or dinner. It was a wonderful south-facing room with views towards the fields and hills.

There was a huge hall with a main staircase which was used by the family. It had family portraits on the walls going up to the first floor bedrooms where the family slept.

There was a further staircase leading up to the second floor and the former nursery rooms. The staff used the stone staircase hidden behind a green baize door in the hall to go down to the staff dining rooms, the cellar, utility area and kitchen. The servant's bedrooms were up a steep staircase leading off the kitchen. In the basement was the kitchen which had red tiled floors with a carpet hearth rug, two ranges, one for spit roasting and one for baking and boiling, a dresser, a long table, a couple of chairs and a clock. The kitchen walls were painted blue as it attracted flies and kept them away from the food. Next door to the kitchen was the scullery where the meat and vegetables were prepared. There were copper utensils and two larders, one to store raw meat, the other to keep cooked meat and pastry. Wyn and Betty looked at all of this with awe and thought to themselves that they would never be able to find their way around the house.

After the tour Mrs Danvers told them that they could rest until the morning but would have to be in the kitchen by 5 o'clock the next day to start work. Wyn and Betty jumped with joy at the unexpected break and ran upstairs to their bedroom to get changed out of their uniforms. Once they were dressed they ran down the back stairs to the kitchen door and out into the sunshine. 'Which way shall we go?' asked Betty.

'Let's head towards those trees and see what is on the other side,' replied Wyn.

They ran towards the trees and stopped. On the other side of the trees was a path across a field which lead to a small village.

It was the beginning of spring and there was green wheat in the fields, violets under the hedges and willows beside the small stream that ran alongside the edge of the trees. They walked across the field into the small village. They could see a few cottages near the inn. A little further away they saw the church and a schoolhouse. The cottages had thatched roofs, whitewashed walls and paned windows. The majority of the houses were constructed of stone or brick and had slated roofs. As it was a warm day, all the windows were open to let fresh air in and there were pies cooling on the window sills of a couple of the houses.
'You don't see that in London,' remarked Betty.
The road carried on round the corner where there was a market place. It being a Sunday there were no stalls out and the whole village was quiet. There wasn't a soul around that Wyn or Betty could see.
'Well,' said Wyn, 'this is going to be a quiet summer if this is what this place is like.'
'You're right,' replied Betty, 'what are we going to do on our days off? Let's just carry on walking and see what's outside the village.'
They carried on walking down the road past hedges thick with berries. There were trees overhanging the road which gave the road a dark shady look. Although it was quite a main road, there was very little traffic although they could hear a train in the distance and could just see a wisp of smoke rising over the trees. They could see the rabbits running in the fields and caught a glimpse of a fox as it ran nervously into the undergrowth. These were sights that Wyn hadn't seen since she had left her home and it was making her feel very sad.

'What's wrong?' asked Betty.
'I'm just missing my home and my mother,' replied Wyn, 'it's just making me want to go home.'
Betty gave no reply, just put her arm around her and carried on walking.
They walked past a clearing in the trees and could see the tops of caravans there.
'Oh Betty!' exclaimed, 'who's that?' 'I've never seen anything like that before.'
'They're gypsies,' replied Wyn, 'we used to get them at home.'
'How exciting,' said Betty, 'let's go and see them.'
They walked towards the three painted caravans. There were three men sitting around a fire smoking and making the clothes pegs they took to the market and tried to sell and the women, who were obviously their wives, were sitting further away and were making cabbage nets. There were children running around screaming and dogs barking.
'What do you want?' they were asked.
'Do you want to buy some pegs?' the man asked and showed them the pegs he had made.
'No thanks,' replied Betty. The gypsy man's face darkened threateningly, 'but we will buy some lucky heather,' said Wyn quickly before he could say anything. She had had experience of their dark side before. Wyn handed over the money and took the heather from the gypsy woman.
'Come on Betty, she said we have to get back now.
They turned and ran back the way they had come. After a while they stopped to get their breath.
'That was an experience I've never had before,' said Betty.

'Now you know to stay away from gypsies', Wyn told her. 'They're a bit on the scary side, they have their own way of living and don't understand ours.'
It was starting to get dark and they were both a bit frightened now because they weren't sure where they were. Do you recognise anything?' Betty asked Wyn.
'No,' replied Wyn, 'but this must be the way we came. We didn't turn round.'
They started seeing shadows in the trees and there were strange animal calls that were making them jump.
Suddenly a hand touched Wyn on the shoulder and she screamed.
'It's only me,' laughed William, 'I didn't mean to make you jump. Mrs Davis sent me out to look for you as it's getting dark and you hadn't come back.'
When Wyn's heartbeat had finally returned to normal, she slapped William on the arm and told him that he had scared the life out of her.
'Me too,' said Betty.
'Sorry,' he replied, 'I didn't mean to scare you. Come on, it's this way.'
By the time they got back to the house it was time for dinner.
'Where have you been?' asked Mrs Davis, 'I thought you were going to miss dinner. Sit down all of you before my cooking gets cold.'
'We've been exploring a bit,' replied Wyn.
'Yes and we saw some gypsies,' said Betty. 'See the lucky heather we bought.'

'Lucky heather, that's a joke,' said Mrs Davis. 'Bet nothing good comes of having that.' They told them all that they had seen and done.

'Next time we'll all go,' William said. 'I fancy having a look around myself, especially at the inn.'

'Don't you take these girls in there,' Mrs Davis told him. 'They're too young.'

William just winked at Wyn and didn't reply. 'Right,' Mrs Davis said, 'it's time you took yourselves off to bed. I want you both down here at 6 o'clock sharp in the morning, so get some sleep and don't be late, there's a lot to do even if we are in the country.'

At 6 o'clock the next morning the two girls were downstairs ready for work. As there were fewer servants in the country house, they had to double up and do the duties of a parlour maid as well as their own. After they had finished lighting the kitchen fires and had cleaned the kitchen, they had to go and sweep and dust the upstairs rooms as well as make the beds of the rest of the household. They also had to make sure each room had soap, towels, writing paper and candles. One of the rooms Wyn went into was where Catherine Brompton slept. She was the nineteen year old daughter of Hester and Charles and was very outspoken and strong willed. The servants of the house had been instructed to call her Miss Catherine. Her bedroom was always very messy with clothes thrown everywhere. She always insisted in walking outside alone, even to the village, although she knew she should have a chaperone. She had the very fashionable seventeen inch waist and her clothes were the latest fashion of fragile gauze dresses covered with bows or flowers. Wyn couldn't understand how she could only wear them once or twice and then throw them away. It just didn't seem right but then that was typical of a spoilt rich girl.

The room next to hers was used by her Mother, Hester. Wyn liked this room it always smelt of lavender and was neat and tidy. All she had to do in there was change the bed and take the dresses left out down to the laundry so they could be pressed. Hester's clothes were generally ready-made and were dresses made of satins, silks, and heavy velvets. My mother would look good in these Wyn thought although she knew that would never happen. These sort of clothes were only for the rich not for the wife of a Welsh fisherman. She sighed and moved on to the next room.

This was the room of Charles Brompton. This was as bad as his daughter's room. There were clothes strewn everywhere. Like his wife and daughter, he was also dressed in the height of fashion. During the day he wore a Norfolk jacket with tweed or woollen breeches. He also had the current facial fashion of being clean shaven. He wore a dinner jacket in the evenings and was considered to be a very smart fashionable man. Wyn quite admired the way he looked although he did frighten her with his sharp tongue on occasions.

When Wyn had finished in his room she walked out onto the landing and bumped into William. 'Well hello,' he said. 'I haven't seen much of you today. I missed you. When are you having a break? We could meet up for a cuddle.'

He said this with twinkle in his eye as he knew it embarrassed her.

Wyn just smiled shyly, 'I don't know, we are so busy today,' she replied.

'Just come and find me,' instructed William, 'we can sneak off somewhere for a while because I want to find out more about you. You've got some sort of a secret in your life and I'm curious. Why did you have to leave Wales when you were so young?'

Wyn just smiled and walked down the stairs to meet Betty. 'What was that all about?' asked Betty. 'I'll tell you later,' replied Wyn, as they heard Mrs Davis shouting them and they had to run the rest of the way to the kitchen. It was lunch time so the kitchen was very busy. As Wyn was the scullery-maid she had to help Mrs Davis by peeling all the vegetables and there always seemed to be a lot of them. She was lucky she had a good friend in Betty, the kitchen maid, and a kindly cook in Mrs Davis as they were teaching her to do more of the cooking so that she could get a better position and have a much easier life. As there was less staff for the house Wyn and Betty had to wait on the other staff in the kitchen before they could sit down and have their own lunch. This was a small break for them because after their lunch they had to help clear away all the dishes from the upstairs dining room and wash and dry them. The floors in the dining room then had to be swept and cleaned again.

When all the work was done and Wyn and Betty had a few minutes break, Betty turned to Wyn and asked her what William was talking to her about earlier.

'He thinks I have a secret reason why I went to London and started work so young,' replied Wyn.

'Well have you,' asked Betty.

'I can't tell you, it's too horrible and I don't want to talk about it,' replied Wyn.

'So there is something,' said Betty. 'You can tell me. I'm not likely to tell him am I?'

Wyn just shook her head.

'Alright,' said Betty seeing the tears in Wyn's eyes, 'but I'm here if you need me.'

Betty wasn't the most intelligent of people but even she could see how upset Wyn was becoming.

They were busy with their jobs for the rest of the day and it wasn't until after dinner was finished that Wyn had any more time to herself. It was a nice warm evening and she went outside into the courtyard to get some fresh air.

William found her there and pulled her into the shadows where no-one could see them. He pulled her close to him and started kissing her. The warm tingling feeling started travelling up her body again.

'Don't,' she said, 'we can't do this it's wrong.'

'Why?' William asked. 'How can anything that feels this nice be wrong?'

'It just is,' replied Wyn. 'I have to go inside. Mrs Davis will be looking for me.'

Sure enough they heard Wyn being called in.

'Until next time,' said William 'giving her another quick kiss.'

That night in bed Wyn told Betty what had happened with William again.

'You have to keep saying no to him,' she said. 'You can't give in, you could end up in big trouble. You don't want to end up in the family way do you?'

'No,' replied Wyn, 'I certainly don't. My mum and dad are decent people and they would be so disappointed in me if that happened. My half- brother Henry has already disgusted my dad, although mum doesn't know about him.'
'What did he do?' asked Betty.
'It doesn't matter,' said Wyn, 'we should get some sleep now.'
Betty lay in the dark and tried to imagine what could have happened in Wyn's family. She gave up after a while and thought that Wyn would tell her when she was ready.

CHAPTER FOUR

Wyn admired Miss Catherine, who was a very pretty girl with shiny reddish brown hair and a slim curvy body. She was very spoilt and treated other people with total disdain. She would go down to the stables every day to ride her horse Crumpet. She had become very close to the groom Frank Cooper who was twenty years old. They could spend a lot of time together as her parents didn't really notice or care what she was doing.

One day Wyn was passing the stables on her way to collect some eggs from the chicken houses when she heard giggling coming from inside. She crept to the door and saw Miss Catherine. She was looking at Frank with a provocative, challenging smile. Frank was a man who was used to being in control, certainly as far as women were concerned, but Wyn knew that he wouldn't be able to or want to resist Catherine. The attraction was just too strong. She wanted him and he wanted her, and damn the consequences. Wyn knew she should move away but just couldn't. She had to know what happened. Catherine leaned back into Frank's embrace. Frank let his hand rest against hers, judging her reaction. She moved her fingers slowly until they were intertwined with his. He dropped her hand then slowly lowered his face to hers to kiss her. As they kissed she slipped her hands under his jacket and around his waist, pulling him closer. She moaned as he explored her mouth with his tongue. He moved his hands over her body through the material of her riding clothes until he reached her breasts, tickling her nipples with his fingers. At this point Wyn decided she had seen enough.

Oh my, she thought this is not good. There's going to be trouble when this comes out.

Wyn picked up the eggs and went back to the house.

'Where have you been?' asked Mrs Davis. 'Did you lay them yourself? You have been gone so long.'

'I'm sorry,' replied Wyn, 'I just got carried away by the sight of the sunset and forgot the time. I could only find seven eggs. They've hidden them well this time.'

Betty walked past Wyn and gave her a puzzled look.

'Were you with William?' she asked. 'No,' replied Wyn 'wait until I tell you what I saw out there.'

'What?' asked Betty.

'I'll tell you when we're in bed,' said Wyn.

Later that night when they were in bed, Wyn told Betty what she had seen in the stables.

'Oh lord,' said Betty, 'that means trouble.'

'That's what I thought,' replied Wyn. 'What should we do?'

'Nothing,' exclaimed Betty. 'We know absolutely nothing about it, although we'll watch what they are doing. Forewarned is forearmed after all.'

'They looked like they were feeling such passion though,' said Wyn, 'just like in books. I want to feel like that one day.'

'Don't you ever touch yourself down there?' asked Betty pointing to her lower body.

Wyn looked at her with a shocked expression. 'No, of course not.'

'You should try it,' Betty told her.

She threw back the bed covers and pulled up her night gown. Just put your finger on this bit here and move it round in circles. She started moving her finger on the nub of her sex and moaned. Wyn felt a strange excitement go through her and pulled her own night gown up. She put her finger where Betty had shown her and started moving it around in a circle. Oh, she thought, that feels so nice. She could hear Betty moaning louder and it made her move her finger faster. Betty cried out one last time and Wyn could feel her own body starting to tense and then it exploded in a mass of pleasure.

'Oh my,' Wyn said, 'I didn't realise that could happen.' Betty was lying back with a smile on her face. 'That's just the best feeling,' she said, 'I love doing that. You can't get into trouble doing it either. Go to sleep now. We have to be up early in the morning.'

The next day it sounded like a bomb had gone off somewhere. Charles Brompton was shouting and when Wyn and Betty ran outside they saw Frank lying prone on the ground. Charles was standing over him with a shotgun. Miss Catherine was there screaming and crying, 'don't kill him daddy please, I love him.'

'Get away from here,' Charles shouted, 'I'm going to teach him a lesson for daring to touch my daughter.'

Hester Brompton ran out and stood in front of her husband blocking his view of Frank. She told Wyn to quickly go and find William, 'tell him to come now, I need him.' Wyn quickly ran off and found William in the kitchen having a cup of tea.

'Come quick William,' said Wyn, 'there's trouble outside.' William ran out and Hester told him to pick Frank up and take him to the stables. Wyn and Betty were to go with them as they might be able to help.

'No,' shouted Charles 'you're not to take him, I'm going to kill him, he dared to touch my daughter.'

'Don't be silly Charles,' said Hester, 'you can't do that in front of so many people. Come inside, we'll decide what to do with him and Catherine.'

William carried the prone Frank into the stables. Wyn and Betty walked in behind them. William put Frank down on the table and stripped his jacket and shirt off. There were deep cuts to the upper part of his body and a huge bruise on the top of his head. Wyn went to the water butt and soaked the piece of cloth she had found. As she went back to the table Frank started coming round. He tried to get off the table but William held him down.

'Stay there you idiot,' he told him. 'You're lucky that Mrs Brompton stopped him shooting you.'

'Where's Catherine?' Frank asked.

'She's in the house with her parents,' said William. 'If I were you I wouldn't even think about her any more. You've been an idiot.

'But we love each other,' said Frank.

'Don't be so stupid,' replied William, 'if you think she'll give all this up for you, you're greatly mistaken.'

Wyn and Betty had cleaned Frank up the best they could when Hester Brompton walked into the stables. 'Could all of you please leave,' she asked, 'I want to talk to Frank.' They didn't know what was said but twenty minutes later Hester walked out followed slowly by Frank. 'I'm leaving,' he told them. 'They're sending Catherine away to a Finishing School in Europe and I've been dismissed.' He groaned and cried out, 'I will never see her again.' He went up to his room above the stables and came down with his possessions about forty minutes later.

'Where will you go?' asked Wyn.

'I've a brother up north,' he replied. 'That'll be a start. Be seeing you.' Then he walked away.

Wyn, Betty and William went back to the house. As they entered the kitchen they could hear Miss Catherine crying and shouting at her mother.

'I'm not going,' she was saying. 'I want to be with Frank.' There was the sound of a slap as the screaming got hysterical. Mrs Brompton came down to the kitchen as she knew there was laudanum in the chest down there. She asked Betty to take it upstairs and give a small amount to Miss Catherine to try and calm her down. When Betty came back she said, 'Miss Catherine is in a real state, all red and blotchy where she has been crying so much, but she's calming down now she has had the laudanum.'

When they got up in the morning they were all asked see Miss Catherine off after breakfast as she was travelling to Europe straight away. They all stood at the bottom of the stairs as Miss Catherine came down. She walked past them with her head lowered. William was taking her and her mother to the station where she was being put onto a train to London. She was to be met by Charles Brompton's spinster sister who was going to accompany her to Europe.

'She looks so sad,' Wyn commented to Betty as she walked past them.

'Embarrassed more like,' replied Betty. 'She thought she was so much better than us but now knows she isn't.'

'I don't think it was like that,' Wyn told her, 'I think Miss Catherine really loved Frank. She's not as snobby as the rest of her family. I think she genuinely liked me. We got on really well. I do feel sorry for her.'

'You're such a romantic idiot,' Betty exclaimed, 'she would never have given up her pampered life to live with a groom.'

When they were in bed that night, instead of just pulling up her own night gown, Betty turned to Wyn and started kissing her. Wyn sat up shocked, 'what are you doing?' she exclaimed. Betty pulled her back onto the bed, 'instead of us just doing it to ourselves, why don't we try doing it to each other?' she asked. 'We can't have a man, so this might be the next best thing. She kissed Wyn again. Wyn opened her mouth to let her slip her tongue in. Betty started exploring with her tongue and at the same time she started touching Wyn's nipple. 'Ooh,' Wyn moaned, 'that feels nice.'

'Touch me as well,' Betty whispered.

Wyn took hold of one of Betty's nipples and squeezed. Betty moaned and moved her hand further down Wyn's body. Wyn moved around to give Betty better access.

They were passionately kissing and touching each other by now. They both could feel the waves of pleasure starting to rise and just let it wash over them.

'Oh that felt so good,' Wyn told Betty 'but is it really bad of us?'

'Yes it did,' replied Betty 'and who cares if it's bad, we can do it whenever we want and it makes us feel really nice. Who's going to know?'

The following day Wyn was in the kitchen as normal when Mrs Danvers the Housekeeper walked in.

'Where's Mrs Davis?' she asked.

'She's in the herb garden,' replied Wyn.
'Can you tell her we need to discuss the menus for the Mayday Hunt. The family are expecting several guests that day and after all that has happened recently, we need to put on a good show,' said Mrs Danvers.
Wyn nodded and carried on peeling the potatoes for dinner. That sounds exciting she thought, I wonder how much of the hunt we will be able to see. She had seen a hunt before in Wales and knew how exciting it could get. She said to Betty, who had just walked into the kitchen, 'we are going to have a hunt for Mayday. Don't you think that is exciting?
I've never seen one,' said Betty. 'You don't get many of those in the east end of London.'
'You'll love it,' said Wyn. 'It will give everyone something else to think about.'
When Mrs Davis came back with the herbs she needed, Wyn told her what Mrs Danvers had said.
'I'll go and see her now,' she said. 'Carry on with the rest of the vegetables until I get back.'
William walked into the kitchen and Wyn told him about the hunt.
'What will you have to do?' she asked him.
'Just look after the guests,' he said. 'The groom has most of the responsibility during a hunt so they better find a new one soon. We might get a chance to go off on our own.'
He winked at her and walked out of the kitchen. Wyn felt a shiver go down her body at the thought of being alone with him. Get a grip of yourself she thought, it won't do to keep thinking like this.

Later that day Wyn saw a lot of activity around the stables. Betty told her that Mr Charles was seeing possible grooms. 'I've seen some very nice lads milling around.' They slipped out of the kitchen and crept round the side of the house heading towards the corner of the stable block to try and see what was happening. They saw Mr Charles with a man of about twenty years old. He had curly blond hair and a rugged face. His body looked very fit and muscular. He wasn't very tall but then most grooms weren't. He mounted Mr Charles's horse Nero who was a very large stallion with a lot of spirit and a mind of his own. He needed a lot of controlling. As the man mounted him, he took off towards the field at high speed.
'Oh no!' exclaimed Wyn, 'he's going to fall off.'
Just as she said that the man got Nero under control and brought him back to Mr Charles. 'Well done lad,' Mr Charles said, 'you did very well with him. You have the job if you want it.'
'Thanks,' said the man, 'I'd like that.'
'Right,' Mr Charles said, 'I'll get William to show you where you sleep and anything else you need to know.'
Wyn and Betty got back to the house just as William was bringing him inside.
'This is Ned Broom,' he said. 'He's the new groom.'
Ned looked at them, 'it's nice to meet all of you,' he said. He looked at Betty in such a way that her cheeks started turning a pink colour.
Wyn nudged her and whispered, 'he likes you.'
'Don't be daft,' replied Betty, 'he's just got here and is getting his bearings.'

'If you say so,' replied Wyn with a smile. 'This summer just got even better. We could all go around together. Four is safer than two.'
Betty just looked at her and exclaimed, 'you're daft you are.'

Mayday finally dawned. Wyn and Betty were so excited because they thought it was going to be such fun. There was going to be a fair, parade, dances, and lots of floral decorations. They had got up very early in the morning and had been out picking flowers to decorate the house with. They heard Mrs Davis shouting and ran to find out what had happened.
'Where are the pies I made earlier?' she asked. 'I put them on the window ledge to cool and now they've gone. Someone around here is stealing food. This isn't the first time it's happened.'
'We haven't seen anything,' Wyn and Betty told her.
'I'm going to see Mrs Danvers,' said Mrs Davis.
'Something strange is happening here.'
Wyn and Betty carried on with the decorations. They wove flowers into garlands and made posies for people to wear and bouquets to fill baskets which were hung on the doors of the house. There was going to be a parade in the village which would be led by a May Queen who was crowned with flowers and attended by several other girls all wearing white, with flowers in their hair, who danced and sang as they followed the May Queen. There were to be dances at the May Fair which would include Morris Dancing which was performed by groups of men dressed in green and white with flowers on their hat. Wyn was really looking forward to going as they had been told they could go for a

couple of hours until they were needed again.

When they had finished with the preparations they were free to go to the village. There was a Maypole decorated with flowers and long ribbons attached to the top. There were children holding on to the ribbons and dancing around the maypole. Wyn and Betty thought it looked wonderful.

'Maybe we can have go later,' said Wyn.

'Don't think so,' replied Betty, 'we have to go back to the house soon.'

Wyn sighed and felt rather sad that they would miss most of the celebrations. There was going to be riding hobby horse races and archery tournaments. The day was to be concluded with a bonfire.

A couple of hours later Wyn and Betty went back to the house. There were horses with riders dressed in their hunting finery just waiting to start. It was very noisy with the riders shouting to each other and the baying of the excited hounds. The horn was blown and then they were off. It was suddenly a lot quieter. William appeared at Wyn's side and asked her if she had been near the stables lately as something strange was happening.

'No,' Wyn told him, 'but it's funny because food has been disappearing from the kitchen. Mrs Davis is very puzzled by it. There has been no sign of any strangers around.'

'Well, it looks like someone has been sleeping in there,' William told her. 'I'm to have a look around and tell you not to wander around the stables on your own in case there is someone around.'

Later they heard Mrs Davis calling them and they went into the kitchen.

'Are all the vegetables peeled?' she asked 'and have you cleaned the floors of the kitchen and scullery?'
'Yes,' Wyn replied.
'Good,' she said, 'the hunt will be back soon and they will be hungry so we need to get started.'
All the preparations were finally finished just as they heard the horn calling the hounds back. 'It's over,' Mrs Davis said. 'They will all be in soon, quick get this food up to the dining room.'
The members of the hunt were being served with a cold buffet. Wyn and Betty spent the next twenty minutes taking the food up to the table. They had just finished when they heard a lot of shouting coming from the stables. William came running into the kitchen.
'What's happened?' asked Wyn?
'You won't believe this, but Frank Cooper has just been found hanging from the stable rafters. He's dead,' he told them.
'Oh my!' exclaimed Mrs Davis, 'I thought he had gone up north to his brothers.'
'So did all of us,' William replied. 'It must have been him that was sleeping in the stables,' 'and stealing the food,' interjected Mrs Davis.
'Poor man,' said Wyn, 'that's so sad. It must have been because of what happened with Miss Catherine. What happens now?' she asked.
'Mr Charles is sending for the Constable and I suppose he will investigate what happened,' William told her.
'Oh Lord,' said Mrs Davis, 'does this mean that what happened with Miss Catherine will have to come out? There will be such a scandal.'

The next day there was a lot of activity around the stables with the Constable and two of his men looking around trying to find out exactly where Frank had been sleeping and if he had left any clue as to why he had hung himself. Suddenly one of the men came running out with a piece of paper in his hands. 'I found this,' he said. He handed it over to the Constable.

'It's a note from Frank Cooper,' he told Mr Charles. 'It says he couldn't stay with his brother and he had no-where else to go, so he came back here but then he decided it was too hard to live anymore so he hung himself. His mind must have been very disturbed,' concluded the Constable. Thank God they all thought, he didn't say anything about Miss Catherine. Mr Charles just gave a huge sigh and said, 'it's such a shame, he was a good groom. I'll make sure he has a decent funeral.'

'If he was such a good groom why did you let him go?' asked the Constable.

'It was a difference of opinion that's all,' Mr Charles replied, 'there was no need for him to do this. I would have given him a decent reference. He would have been able to get another position quite easily.'

Come along,' Mrs Davis said to Wyn and Betty, 'we still have a house full of guests to cater for.

'They don't have to know what has happened here,' said Mr Charles. 'They have had a good day. Let's keep it that way. Mr Carter, the Butler, is looking after them at the moment, giving them plenty to drink, so they will be quite happy.' He turned to William, 'shut the stable door until Frank has been removed. 'Ned is looking after the horses in the paddock. We'll wait until everyone has left before we sort this mess out,' he told him.

Once all the guests had left the, undertakers came and took Frank away. The funeral took place a few days later. Mr Charles had persuaded the vicar to bury Frank in the grave yard even though he had committed the sin of taking his own life. A small buffet was arranged for the rest of the staff in the staff dining room. Mr & Mrs Brompton both made a brief appearance and said a few words to them. Then it was over. It was never to be spoken of again although Wyn and Betty wondered if they had told Miss Catherine. We'll never know Wyn thought. It is all so sad.

CHAPTER FIVE

At last they all had the same day off so Wyn, Betty, William and Ned decided to go into the village together as they had been told that once every summer a German band passed through the village and they would be playing outside the inn. The band was composed of a father and his six sons, the eldest of which played the cornet, the youngest beat the drum. They sat in a circle in green uniforms and played the kind of music none of them had ever heard before although it is was quite entertaining.

'Well, that was different,' remarked William when they had finished. There was also a man with a dancing bear. It danced with a long pole balanced across its front paws and then did exercises at the command of the man.

'Poor thing,' said Wyn, 'look at the state of him.'

His fur was mangy and the smell of him turned their stomachs.

'He's obviously very old,' said Betty. 'You should be ashamed,' she said to the man.

He just gave her an evil look and turned away.

'Let's see what the inn has to offer,' suggested William. They all turned and went inside. The landlord brought them mugs of frothing beer. Wyn and Betty took very small sips of the beer as neither of them had ever tasted it before and they both pulled a face.

'Yuk,' said Betty as she tried taking another sip. 'I suppose I'll get used to it.'

They sat quietly for a minute drinking until they heard shouting coming from outside. They were curious so went outside to have a look and saw a wagon full of household items. The man sitting on top of the wagon was a small, thin-legged old man. He was wearing an old velvet coat with a feather stuck in the band of his battered old hat and he had an old red and yellow neckerchief knotted round his neck. He set his stock out on the ground and rang a bell to get attention. He had all kinds of items for the home for sale from tea cloths to full dinner services. Wyn and Betty ran over to have a look.

'I never realised life in the country was so exciting,' Betty remarked.

They jumped back as women and children started running towards the wagon to see what there was to buy. A fight broke out between two of the women over a set of jugs.

'Now, now you two,' the odd little man said. 'There's another set over here, you can both have one.' The two women went off happy, each holding a set of jugs.

Wyn and Betty walked back over to William and Ned laughing.

'I've never seen anything like that,' said Wyn.

'Me neither,' responded Betty. 'What shall we do now?' she asked.

'There's the small market town of Crampney nearby and it's market day,' said William, 'let's go and see what they've got there. It's not too far to walk.'

They all agreed and walked out of Ripplesdown along the road to Crampney. As it was market day, there were a lot of carts and wagons travelling along the road. They had to keep to the verge where the grass was quite high which made walking difficult.

'Oh my!' exclaimed Wyn after tripping again. 'This is not easy walking.'

'Come on,' replied William smiling, 'stop moaning and just walk.'

'It's alright for you,' she replied 'you haven't got your best shoes on. I don't want to spoil them.'

The traffic on the road eased so they could walk in the road for a bit which made the going easier.

In the distance they could see the spire of the church and knew they were getting closer to the town.

'I think we'll find an inn first,' said William. 'I could do with a bite to eat and a drink.' They all readily agreed and walked into the town. They could see crowds of people walking down rows of stalls with all kinds of goods for sale. Wyn started feeling quite excited by everything she was seeing.

'Come on,' said William, 'let's find the inn first, I'm really thirsty, then we'll go explore. It looks like there is going to be a lot to see.'

They sat down in the inn which was full of people. There was a lot of talking as most of the customers of the inn were there to sell their goods and prices were being argued about. They drank their beer which was very welcome as they were all very thirsty. As soon as they were finished they went outside into the sunshine.

There were market stalls selling all kinds of goods from fruit and vegetables to the meat stalls. The fish market was hidden from view although you could still smell where it was. Further up the hill were the pens for the livestock market. They were full of lambs, calves and pigs waiting to be sold. Wyn felt quite sorry for them. They walked all around the town. There were cottages with railings enclosing their front gardens which were full of flowers.

There was the railway station and shops. It took them a long time to walk around. As they walked down the main street they saw a man on a penny farthing.
'I don't think I could ever ride on one of those do you?' Wyn asked them.
William was watching fascinated. 'I want one,' he said.
'Me too,' said Ned, 'it looks like fun. I don't know how he stays on it.'
All too soon it was time to start making their way home. It was getting towards dusk and the sun was starting to set. It was quite a long walk back. They had bought some bread and cheese and decided to eat it by the side of a little brook sitting with their feet in the water. When all the bread and cheese had gone William said, 'come on we've got to get back before it's really dark.' They started walking again but they were getting tired and slower.
'We've got to rest,' Wyn exclaimed, 'I'm so tired.'
'Alright,' William agreed, 'let's just go over there and sit under the trees.'
They all walked off the road into the field running alongside the road. It was a lot darker by now and they were finding it hard to see their way. William sat down next to Wyn. Ned and Betty had walked further away. William put his arm around Wyn and drew her towards him. She didn't stop him when he raised her face to his and kissed her gently. She felt a shiver run down her back. William intensified the kiss, putting his tongue in her mouth. It felt a lot different from the kisses she and Betty shared but it was much nicer, although she liked what she and Betty did. She could feel the whiskers on his face scrapping against her cheek and there were wonderful

sensations building in her body but she remembered Betty's warning about getting into trouble. She pulled away from him.

'What's wrong?' asked William in a husky voice.

'I can't,' replied Wyn, 'it's wrong. Let's just get back now.'

She was just going to call to Betty when she heard a very loud slapping noise and Betty came running out of the shadows. She put her arm through Wyn's.

'Come on,' she cried 'let's go.'

'Betty,' shouted Ned, 'I'm sorry, I thought you wanted to.'

'Well now you know,' replied Betty as she and Wyn went back onto the road and started walking. It seemed to take a long time but they finally saw the house ahead of them. Wyn turned to William and kissed him on the cheek, 'thank you for a very nice day,' she said 'I had a very nice time.'

'Me too,' replied William, 'we'll have to find somewhere else to go next time.'

'I'd like that,' said Wyn.

She turned in time to see Ned giving Betty a quick kiss. When Wyn and Betty were in their room Betty told Wyn that something strange had happened when she had gone to meet Ned at the stables. 'I'm sure I saw Frank Cooper.'

'You can't of,' replied Wyn, 'he's dead, we saw his body.'

'I know,' replied Betty, 'but it really looked like him.'

'Maybe you've started seeing ghosts,' suggested Wyn laughing.

Betty just shrugged and said that she was probably just seeing things and that it wasn't worth worrying about. She then asked Wyn what had happened between her and William in the dark. 'He just kissed me,' replied Wyn, 'but it started feeling too nice so I stopped him. What happened with you and Ned?'

'Ned went too far,' replied Betty, 'he put his hand on my breast so I slapped him. We were friends by the time we got back though, so we can all go out again the next time we all have a day off together as it was fun wasn't it?'

'Yes,' replied Wyn, 'I enjoyed myself. I really like William.'

Once they were in bed they talked more about the day and all the things they had done.

'I liked sitting in the Inn,' said Wyn, 'that was the first time I've ever been inside one.'

'Me too,' replied Betty, 'when's our next day off? I can't wait.'

'Not for a couple of weeks,' Wyn told her.

'Oh that's too long, I like going out with you, William and Ned.'

'You just want more kisses,' said Wyn, 'me too.'

They lay back and talked about what they might let William and Ned do next time they were alone, getting quite excited in the process. They started to touch themselves and each other again. They were learning about each other's and their own bodies and the pleasure they were feeling was getting more intense.

'I did enjoy kissing William,' Wyn told Betty as Betty starting really kissing her, 'but this is so nice too. I really want to feel his body on mine but I know it's not the right thing to do yet.'

She moaned as Betty moved her fingers lower and pushed one right inside Wyn moving it in and out, at the same time rubbing the nub of her sex. Wyn could feel the pleasure building, 'turn around,' she told Betty huskily, 'I want to taste you.' Betty quickly turned around and Wyn used her tongue until she felt the wetness and heard the cry as Betty's pleasure climaxed.

A few weeks later Wyn and Betty were walking around the estate, as they had a rare couple of hours off, when they came across an old barn.

'Let's go in,' suggested Betty, 'I've never been inside a barn before.'

They went in and were disappointed that there were just bales of hay. Betty spotted a ladder leading up to another level.

'I'm going to see what's up there,' she told Wyn.

'Be careful,' Wyn replied. 'There could be spiders and mice up there.'

'Ugh I'll be careful,' said Betty.

She climbed up the ladder and disappeared from sight. A few minutes later she called down, 'come up Wyn, it's an amazing view from up here.'

Wyn climbed the ladder, looked through the hatch that Betty was looking through and stood staring in wonder at the view in front of her. They could see for miles across the countryside from up there. There were cows and sheep in the fields and they could even see the glimmer of water on a stream in the distance.

'Ooh it's lovely,' whispered Wyn. 'So peaceful and quiet.'

They sat with their legs dangling out of the hatch and just looked at everything in front of them. Suddenly there was a sound from down below and they both jumped.

'What's that?' whispered Wyn.

'I don't know,' replied Betty. She eased herself towards the edge of the floor and looked down. Wyn heard her gasp and edged her way forward to join her. Betty put her finger to her lips and whispered 'shh.' She pointed down. Wyn looked down and saw Mr Charles down there with the farmer's wife, Annie. 'Oh,' she mouthed to Betty. As they watched, Mr Charles took Annie into his arms and started kissing her passionately. They sank onto a hay bale and Mr Charles started undressing Annie. He undid her blouse and exposed her voluptuous breasts. He moved his fingers over her nipples and she gasped. His hand moved further down her body and he pulled her skirt off. She wasn't wearing any kind of under garment and her womanhood was immediately exposed. 'Undo me,' Mr Charles moaned. Annie undid his shirt and ran her hands over his chest, her fingers mingling with his hair. She tugged on his nipples and he gave a loud moan. 'Lower,' he gasped as her hand started moving further down his body. She undid his trousers and his member sprang out. Wyn and Betty gaped at it in surprise. It was very large and erect. They looked at each other and had to stop themselves from laughing out loud. Mr Charles moaned louder as Annie put her hand around him and started moving it up and down. 'Stop, stop,' moaned Mr Charles 'or it'll be over too soon.' He moved on top of her and started putting small kisses all down her body until he got to the heart of her sex. He moved his tongue around in circles and Annie's body arched in pleasure. 'Oh quick,' she said, 'get inside me, I'm ready.' Mr Charles got on top of her, inserted his member inside her and started moving up and down moving faster and faster. Annie was moaning in pleasure until she suddenly cried out as she climaxed. Charles immediately pulled out of her body and she moved down to take him into her mouth. Mr Charles had hold of her head pushing himself backwards and forwards in her mouth faster and faster. He suddenly went still and then his body started jerking in pleasure. He cried out loudly. It all went quiet and Mr Charles gave Annie a long kiss. 'That was wonderful,' he told her. They lay down together in a satisfied silence.

Wyn and Betty were getting concerned as they had been in the barn for a long time and knew they had to be back in to the house shortly. They looked at each other but couldn't say anything because the two people down below would hear them. They just had to lay there and wait. Just then there was a noise coming from outside the barn and Mr Charles and Annie jumped up.

'Be quiet,' he told her, 'I'll go and see what it is. Give it a few minutes then leave.'

He gave her a kiss goodbye and left. Annie waited until she could hear whoever it was moving away with Mr Charles and then she walked out of the barn. Wyn looked at Betty and they both started giggling.

'Oh my,' exclaimed Wyn, 'did you see the size of that?'

'It was almost purple on the end,' laughed Betty.

'What about the size of Annie's breasts,' said Wyn.

'I've never seen ones that big,' agreed Betty. She pulled up her blouse and said, 'look at these, they're so small compared to hers.'

'Maybe,' replied Wyn taking a nipple into her mouth, 'but they are just right for me.'

'Stop that,' Betty replied. 'We have to get back to the house.'

She adjusted her clothes and they walked to the door of the barn, looked out to make sure no-one was there and ran giggling back to the house.

'Where have you two been?' asked Mrs Davis, 'I need the two of you to peel the vegetables for dinner and set the table upstairs. Come on get on with it.'

Wyn and Betty went into the pantry to get the vegetables then took them into the scullery the start peeling them. While they were doing it, they couldn't help talking about what they had seen in the barn.

'It made me feel all funny inside,' Wyn confided to Betty, 'I really want to feel what it's like with William.'

'Yes well I'd like to know how it feels with Ned too, but we can't do it with any man until we are betrothed to them, and even then we'd have to be careful.'

'Maybe we could do what Annie did for Mr Charles, nothing would happen then,' suggested Wyn.

'Yeah,' replied Betty, 'but you'd have to trust them to stop before anything happened.'

'Stop whispering and get on with your work,' shouted Mrs Davis.

They smiled at each other and carried on peeling vegetables.

After dinner they met up with William and Ned. They had decided not to tell them what they had seen in the barn as they thought it might give them ideas. As Wyn and William linked arms, Ned and Betty did the same and they all decided to walk around the estate as it was a nice night. They talked about all the things they wanted to do on their

next day off which was coming up the following Sunday. As the weather wasn't very warm anymore, they didn't have much choice so had just decided to spend time in the local inn. They walked into the trees and Betty and Ned walked off in front. William pulled Wyn into his arms and kissed her passionately. He put his hand on her breast and started rubbing, Wyn felt a sensation go all the way to her sex. She didn't stop him this time and his hand started moving lower. Wyn moaned and moved her hand over his chest. It felt hard and strong. William started to breathe a bit heavier as Wyn's hand moved further down his body and brushed against his hard cock. She started to move her hand up and down through his clothes. 'Oh he,' moaned, 'don't stop, stroke harder.' She moved her hand harder and faster against him and could feel his body starting to tense. 'Faster,' he cried, 'keep going.' She moved her hand faster and he suddenly tensed and then cried out as his body exploded. 'Oh Wyn,' he said, 'that was wonderful. I've never felt like that before.'
Just then they heard Betty and Ned coming back towards them. 'We better get back,' Betty told them. 'It must be getting near bed time.'
'Can we come with you?' asked William winking at Wyn, 'going to bed sounds good.'
'Don't be so rude,' Betty told him laughingly.
When they were in bed that night Wyn asked, 'what did you and Ned get up to when you were by yourselves?' Betty told her that Ned had taken her into the trees and kissed her hard. 'How did that feel?' asked Wyn,
'Oh it was really nice. I let him touch my breasts as well, he made my nipples go very hard and I felt like I wanted

him to go further. I could feel how hard it made him as he pressed against me.'

'That's nothing,' Wyn told her, 'William starting kissing me passionately and feeling my breasts. He touched me everywhere and I put my hands all over his body. I touched his hard cock through his trousers and made him cry out in pleasure.'

'Oh my!' exclaimed Betty, 'you went a lot further than me and Ned.'

'Well,' replied Wyn, 'seeing Mr Charles and Annie made me feel quite excited but William didn't touch me, so I still feel like that.'

'Me too,' said Betty. 'Come here.'

Afterwards they lay there quietly talking. 'I don't know why more women don't do what we do because it feels so nice and its safe,' remarked Betty.

'Maybe they do,' replied Wyn, 'how would we know?

'Maybe all women do this until they are wed. It's alright for men, they don't have to worry about babies like we do. That's why I think maybe this is normal for us women,' said Betty. 'It doesn't stop me wanting William,' though Wyn replied.

'No I must admit,' said Betty, 'I still want to feel Ned inside me, hopefully soon.'

CHAPTER SIX

It was a couple of weeks later when Ned came running into the kitchen shouting for them to get Mr Carter.

'What's up?' asked Mrs Davis.

'I really need to speak to Mr Carter,' replied Ned.

Mr Carter came rushing into the kitchen, 'what's all the noise about?'

'Nero, Mr Charles's horse has come galloping back to the stables,' Ned told him breathlessly, 'Mr Charles wasn't on him.'

'Oh no!' exclaimed Mr Carter. 'Quickly all of you, get everyone you can find to go out and look around the estate for Mr Charles, I'll go and tell Mrs Brompton what's happened.'

Ned ran back outside to see who he could find.

'Take your aprons off,' Mrs Davis told Wyn and Betty, 'go and help look for Mr Charles.' Wyn and Betty did as she told them and then ran out of the house.

When they got outside, Wyn turned to Betty and asked if she thought this had got anything to do with what they had seen in the barn.

'I don't know,' replied Betty, 'I think we should keep quiet about that for now. This might not be anything to do with that so we might be dropping Mr Charles and Annie right in it. We'll just have to see how things go. Let's go towards the barn now and see if there is any sign of Mr Charles there.'

They walked across the estate towards the barn, looking all around them as they walked in case there were any signs on the ground. They had seen nothing by the time they got to the barn. They walked inside and looked all around the ground floor but, without moving all the hay bales, they couldn't see much.

'We'll have to get William and Ned to try and move some of these,' Wyn said.

'Let's try up the ladder,' Betty suggested. 'I'll go first.'

Betty went up the ladder and told Wyn that there was nothing up there.

'Come on,' she said, 'let's go back and get the others.'

When they got back to the house they found chaos. All the men from the hunt had turned up to help look for Mr Charles and had brought the dogs with them. Mrs Davis was running around the kitchen making tea for them all.

'Quick,' she said, 'get all the cups and saucers you can find. I don't think we'll have enough' she muttered to herself.

Wyn started opening all the cupboards pulling out every cup and saucer she could see.

'Some of the cups don't have saucers,' she told Mrs Davis.

'Don't worry about that,' Mrs Davis replied, 'just put them on the table, they'll just have to rough it today.'

With all the tea made Mrs Davis, Wyn and Betty took all the cups up to the drawing room and handed them around. There was a lot of speculating going on amongst the men as to where Mr Charles could be. Wyn and Betty kept their ears open but it seemed no-one knew of the relationship between Mr Charles and Annie except for them.

After the men had drunk their tea they all filed outside, gave the dogs one of Mr Charles's jackets to smell so they could get his scent and then walked off onto the estate. Wyn and Betty could hear the baying of the hounds as they ran around trying to get the scent. Suddenly they took off with the men running behind them.

'Maybe they've found something,' said Wyn.

'I hope so,' replied Betty, 'I don't really want to have to say anything. We'll wait to tell William and Ned about the barn. We might not need to now.'

William and Ned came back from searching around the stables. 'Nothing,' William said. 'He's not around there.' Wyn told them that the dogs seemed to have got the scent of something.

'Hope so,' Ned said, 'we'll wait here to see what they've found.'

It was a lot later that day before the men came back to the house. All the dogs had found was a piece of Mr Charles's shirt that had been snagged by a tree. Everyone in the house was disappointed as they knew it was now going to be another long day tomorrow. Mr Carter just told them that as it was dark now, they couldn't start looking again until the morning so they might as well just have some dinner and go to bed. Mrs Davis called to Wyn and Betty to come and help her do the dinner as Emily Danvers was going to try and get Mrs Brompton to eat something.

'Peel the vegetables,' she told them, 'but don't do too many as I'm only going to prepare a light meal.

After dinner had been taken up to Mrs Brompton on a tray, Wyn and Betty sat down with William, Ned and Mrs Davis to eat. All the talk was about Mr Charles and what could have happened to him. They asked William and Ned about moving the hay bales in the barn the next day just so they could search underneath them. William and Ned agreed to help them.

'I don't think there'll be anything there,' Wyn told them, 'but we should have a look anyway.'

The next day they walked across the fields to the barn. William and Ned walked in first and started moving the hay bales from one side of the barn to the other. They had got halfway through moving them when Wyn saw something.

'Hang on a minute,' she called out, 'I can see something.' William came over to where she was standing and looked down. They could see part of an arm underneath the bale.

'Oh no,' exclaimed William, 'it looks like we've found Mr Charles. Wyn, run and get Mr Carter and tell him, he'll know what to do.'

Wyn ran back to the house and shouted for Mr Carter. He came out and Wyn told him that they thought they had found Mr Charles. She told him to quickly follow her and they ran back to the barn. He went into the barn and leant down to see what they had found. He then told William and Ned to carefully lift the bale off Mr Charles so that he could see if there were any signs of life. Once the bale had been lifted, Mr Carter leant down to look. He suddenly jumped back and stood staring down in shock at the lifeless body of his employer.

'Take your shirt off and cover Mr Charles up,' he instructed William. He turned to Wyn, 'run back to the house and tell Mrs Davis to send for Constable Wilson as it looks like Mr Charles is dead. Oh yes and tell Mrs Danvers so that she can break the news gently to Mrs Brompton.'

Wyn ran back to the house and down into the kitchen. Mrs Davis was sitting at the table drinking a cup of tea.

'They've found him,' she told her once she had got her breath back. 'Mr Carter says you are to send for Constable Wilson and I need to see Mrs Danvers.'

'She's in her room,' Mrs Davis told her, 'go and tell her while I find someone to go and get the constable.'

Wyn ran up to Mrs Danvers room and knocked on the door. 'Come in,' she was instructed. She walked in and told Mrs Danvers what Mr Carter had said.

'Oh dear,' replied Mrs Danvers, 'I can't begin to imagine what will happen now. Run along now and go and get yourself a cup of tea, you have done enough for one day.'

By the time Wyn got back to the kitchen Betty, William and Ned were there. They had a pot of tea on the table and Wyn got a cup and saucer and helped herself. She and Betty looked at each other and nodded.

'What do you two know?' asked William.

Wyn told them about what they had seen and heard in the barn.

'You'll have to tell Constable Wilson' William told them.

'We know,' Betty said.

The next few hours were chaotic when the constable and a couple of his men turned up. They went up to the barn and had a good look at Mr Charles. The Undertaker had been sent for and turned up with his hearse. He and his assistants put Mr Charles into a temporary coffin and took him away. When Constable Wilson came back to the house after inspecting the barn, he told them that Mr Charles had been killed with a sickle so it was definitely murder. He asked to see Mrs Brompton. Mrs Danvers took him upstairs to the drawing room. After a few minutes they could hear Mrs Brompton sobbing loudly.

'Put the kettle on,' Mrs Davis told Betty, 'I think some very sweet tea will be needed.'

It was a long time before Mrs Danvers returned slowly into the kitchen.

'Take a cup of sweet tea up to the drawing room,' she told Wyn, 'give it to Mrs Brompton but don't speak to her, she needs time alone.'

Wyn took the cup upstairs. Mrs Brompton was sitting in a chair by the window just staring out. Her face was tear streaked and pale and she was holding a very wet handkerchief. Wyn put her tea down on the small table next to the chair. She had a clean handkerchief in her pocket so she prised the wet one out of Mrs Brompton's hand and gave her the clean one. Mrs Brompton didn't move or even acknowledge her presence so Wyn just left the room.

When Wyn got back downstairs she told Betty that Mrs Brompton was in a bad way.

'It's to be expected' Betty said, 'her husband has just been murdered.'

'I know,' replied Wyn, 'but it just makes me feel so sad for her. What about Miss Catherine, who's going to tell her?'

'I don't know,' Betty said, 'I suppose someone will send a telegraph to the school.'

'Poor Miss Catherine,' Wyn remarked, 'not only has she lost her lover but now her father has been murdered.'

'Just as well Frank Cooper's dead, he would be the main suspect otherwise,' Betty suggested.

'I suppose he would,' agreed Wyn, 'you don't suppose the murder is related to that somehow do you?'

'No,' replied Betty, 'I think it's more to do with Annie. We better go and see Constable Wilson and tell him what we saw.'

They both went outside to find the constable. They found him in deep discussions with Ned by Nero's stable.

'We think there's something you need to know,' Wyn said. 'Oh yes, what's that?' asked Constable Wilson looking at both of them intently. Betty told him what she and Wyn had seen. 'That's very interesting,' he remarked. 'I think I'd better go and talk to farmer Jenkins.'

The farmer's name was Horace Jenkins but he was known to the villagers as Horrid Horace as he was not the nicest person in the village and was rude to almost everyone he came across. He was also extremely bad tempered and would blow up at the smallest thing. It seemed there was a good chance he could have killed Mr Charles if he had known about Mr Charles and Annie.

Constable Wilson went to see farmer Jenkins and was with him for a long time. When he came back, they all asked him what he thought. It couldn't have been farmer Jenkins,' he told them, 'he and Annie were on a neighbouring farm all that day and the farmer confirmed it.' 'Does he know about Annie and Mr Charles?' Wyn asked him.

'No,' he replied, 'I didn't think he needed to know, it would just cause more problems.' They all breathed a large sigh of relief, at least Mrs Brompton would be spared that information, she had enough on her plate. Constable Jenkins now had a huge problem though, after asking around he knew there were dozens of possible suspects as Mr Charles owed money to a lot of people, so he went back to the barn with extra men to see if he could find any other clues.

The next day the Undertaker brought Mr Charles back to the house where he was put into the front parlour in his temporary coffin while the funeral was being arranged. Mr Carter and Mrs Danvers were both helping Mrs Brompton with this as she was too upset to do it on her own. All the relatives had to be informed and cards were written and posted, the cards and the envelopes they were put in, had a black edge to them so that the person receiving them knew that someone had died even before they opened the envelope. Three days later Mr Charles was put into his permanent coffin. The front parlour was already full of flowers that neighbours and villagers had brought to show their respect for Mr Charles and it smelt lovely in there. He was in an open coffin and most of the villagers had come to see him out of curiosity. The Undertaker had done a good job on him and had dressed him in his best morning suit. Mrs Brompton had taken to sitting in there with Mr Charles for hours just talking to him. They all felt very sad for her. There were several tradesmen coming to the house as Mrs Brompton, Miss Catherine and even the servants had to have mourning dress. Mrs Brompton and Miss Catherine were to have dresses made of silk in deepest black with a full black veil, the female servants were also to have black dresses made and the men were to have dark suits along with black gloves, hatbands and cravats. Mrs Davis was also busy making preparations for the funeral tea and the butcher was a frequent visitor to the house. There was to be joints of meat, cider, ale, pies and cakes. She was keeping Wyn and Betty very busy as she had a lot of preparation and cooking to do. 'I'll be very happy when this funeral is over,' she kept telling them.

'So will I,' muttered Betty after Mrs Davis had shouted at her again for some imagined mistake.

CHAPTER SEVEN

A few days later William was sent to the station to pick up Miss Catherine who had come back to attend her father's funeral. There had been no further clues as to who had killed Mr Charles and Constable Wilson had almost given up hope of ever finding the culprit. Wyn was out in the yard when William brought the carriage back.

'How is she?' Wyn asked him.

'She's very upset and hardly said a word the whole journey,' William told her. 'She looks terrible, this has obviously affected her badly.'

Just then a man crept around the corner of the stables.

'Look at that,' whispered Wyn, 'it's the ghost of Frank Cooper that Betty saw.'

'Where?' asked William. The man had gone and William had missed seeing him. 'You and Betty are seeing things,' he added.

'I'm not seeing things,' Wyn retorted, 'I did just see him.'

'It's probably a trick of the light that makes it look like him,' William told her, 'it can't be him, he's dead, I know, I cut the body down.'

Just then Betty shouted for Wyn to go back to the house. Wyn walked back to the house thinking, I did see him, I know I did, it's very strange. When she got back she told Betty what she had seen.

'I thought it was just me,' Betty said, 'maybe we should tell Constable Wilson, he might not think we are seeing things.'

'Yes you're right,' agreed Wyn, 'he probably should know.'

After they had finished their morning duties, they went to find Constable Wilson. They found him back in the barn searching the ground again. Betty told him what she had seen before Mr Charles's death and Wyn told him about seeing the same person again that day.

'That sounds very strange,' agreed Constable Wilson. 'I think I should try and find out more information about Mr Cooper.'

'I think he came from Huddersfield,' Wyn told him.

'I'll send a telegraph to the Constable up there,' he said, 'he might know something about him or his family.'

As they all walked out of the barn, William came running towards them and shouted to Wyn and Betty to get back to the house as Mrs Davis was shouting for them.

'Oh dear,' exclaimed Wyn, 'what's happened now?'

They ran back to the house and Mrs Davis told them that Miss Catherine was in a state because she had seen the ghost of Frank Cooper lurking around the stables.

'We know he's there,' Wyn told her, 'we've both seen him too. I don't really think he's a ghost,' Wyn said, 'he must be real.'

They told Mrs Davis that they informed Constable Wilson about him already and the Constable was going to look into it.

'That's good,' said Mrs Davis, 'I'll go and tell Mrs Danvers so that she can tell Mrs Brompton and Miss Catherine.'

After dinner Wyn and Betty went outside to meet William and Ned. It was getting harder to meet up outside as the weather was getting colder.

'It'll soon be winter,' Betty exclaimed, 'what will we do then?'

'I don't know,' replied Wyn, 'I'm not sure we'll be staying in the country anyway.'

'What'll happen to Ned if we go back to London?' asked Betty in a panic.

'I'm sure Mrs Brompton will need him in London,' Wyn told her.

They walked up to William and Ned and both of them received a long kiss. They told them that Miss Catherine had seen the ghost of Frank Cooper too.

'We've told Constable Wilson and he's looking into it' Wyn said.

'There are some strange things going on around here' William remarked, 'the other day I saw a man I know who works for Sir John Porchester.'

'What's he doing around here?' asked Ned. 'I'd tell Constable Wilson about him too,' William nodded, 'I'll do it tomorrow,' he said, 'but tonight we have better things to do.' 'Where are we going?' Wyn and Betty asked.

'We thought we might walk to the village Inn,' Ned told them. 'It's not going to be easy to get there when the snow comes so we might as well enjoy it now.'

They started walking briskly towards the village, it was too cold for a slow stroll. The Inn was lovely and warm when they walked in with a roaring fire in the corner. There were four chairs empty in front of the fire so they all sat down.

'This is nice,' commented Wyn.

William got up and went to the bar to buy four beers, while he was up there he started speaking to another man standing on his own at the bar. When he came back he told them that the man he was talking to was the one who worked for Sir John. They all turned round to look but the man had gone.

'That's strange,' William said, 'he still had a full tankard of beer to drink.' He turned to Wyn and Betty and said, 'I don't think you should go anywhere by yourselves until the mystery of who killed Mr Charles has been solved as there are too many mysterious things happening.'

'I don't think I want to,' Wyn remarked.

'Me neither,' Betty agreed.

Then they put it out of their minds as they wanted to have a very happy night.

The next day William went to find Constable Wilson and told him about the man he had seen lurking around the estate. 'This is getting very interesting,' the Constable replied. 'I've gone from no suspects to two of them in a couple of days. Do you know what this man's name is?'

'I'm afraid not,' replied William, 'I only know him to nod to because he works for Sir John Porchester and I work for Mr Charles and they used to meet up sometimes to play cards.'

'I'll have to see what I can find out,' said Constable Wilson. 'One of these men must have something to do with it.'

Just then one of his men came running up. 'What is it?' asked Constable Wilson.

'We've found a campsite where someone has been sleeping. There's a bed of hay with an old blanket on it and old food scraps lying around.'

'Show me where,' instructed Constable Wilson.

William went with them in case an extra person was needed, after all this might be the man who killed Mr Charles. The camp was right at the edge of the estate hidden in the undergrowth. It was situated a long way into a large shrub which gave some protection from the elements. There was no sign that anyone had been back so the Constable told one of his men to stay there hidden amongst the bushes in case whoever it was came back. 'Don't let him see you,' he instructed, 'just see who it is and report back to me.'

He sent his other man back to town to arrange a rota so that they took it in turns to stay and wait. 'Don't worry about staying overnight,' he told them, 'it's getting too cold for that, just concentrate on daylight hours, hopefully it won't be too long before he comes back.' William told him he had to get back to the house as it was the funeral the next day and there was a lot to do.

'Alright,' the Constable said, 'but keep your eyes open for anything else unusual.'

It was finally the day of the funeral and Wyn and Betty had been up since early light as they had to light fires in all the rooms as several relatives would be staying after the funeral. They also had to make sure the rooms were clean and the beds were made. They put flowers in every room to make sure the whole house had the scent of flowers, not of death. After they had finished they then went down to the kitchen to help Mrs Davis finish off the funeral food.

'Hurry up,' Mrs Davis told them, 'finish here and then go and get ready, the funeral guests will start arriving soon. Mrs Brompton will expect to see us outside and ready to go when the hearse arrives.'

Carriages started arriving with the relatives and they were shown into the house by Mr Carter dressed in his black suit. They were shown to their rooms by Mrs Danvers. Once they had settled in, William was waiting to show them into the drawing room where they were given a glass of sherry. The mood was sombre and quiet and any talking was done in soft whispers. The room went silent when Mrs Brompton and Catherine walked in hand in hand. They walked around the room talking quietly to the relatives gathered there. After a few minutes Mrs Danvers came into the room and whispered to Mrs Brompton that the hearse had arrived outside. They walked outside to see the servants all standing in a line in their mourning clothes with their heads bowed. Mrs Brompton and Catherine smiled as they walked past them towards the hearse. It was black with glass sides, it had lots of silver and gold decoration and was filled with flowers. The coffin was covered with a black cloth that was attached to it with brass nails. Six black horses with black ostrich feather plumes on their heads, pulled the hearse.

They got into the first coach behind the hearse and their relatives followed behind in coaches with their blinds drawn. The men were in their full mourning suits and had black bands around their top hats. The women were in black gowns with black veils and black gloves. They held black-edged handkerchiefs to their eyes. Wyn, Betty and the rest of the servants walked slowly behind the coaches as it wasn't far to the church in the village. They went past the villagers who were lined along the narrow road. They all bowed their heads in respect as they went past.

The procession stopped at the church which was in the centre of the cemetery. They all entered the church quietly and sat down with Mrs Brompton and Catherine in the front row and the servants right at the back. Everyone stood as the coffin was carried in and laid on a bier. After a short service everyone walked to the grave where the minister said a few words before committing his body to the grave. Mr Charles was then laid to rest. Wyn and Betty gave sighs of relief when it was all over. With everyone in black and all the crying it had been totally depressing and they were both quite upset.

'We have to pull ourselves together,' Wyn told Betty, 'we've now got a funeral tea to serve.'

'I know,' replied Betty, 'it's going to be hard though.'

'Come on girls,' said Mrs Davis coming up behind them. 'I know it's very sad but we've got things to do, so come on, there will be time to be sad later.'

They walked back to the house briskly as they had to get back before the other funeral guests so that they could lay out the funeral tea in the dining room as, although it was a buffet, this was the largest room.

Once Mrs Davis, Wyn and Betty got back to the house they stripped off their coats, put their aprons on and started work straight away as they knew they didn't have much time before the rest of the guests would be back. Wyn was taking trays of food up to the dining room where Betty was already waiting. She would then spread it out on the tables. There was all kinds of meats and pies. They could choose to carry on drinking sherry or brandy but there was also ale or cider. The villagers would be sitting in the servant's dining room downstairs and would have the same food but they would only be offered ale, cider or gin.

William was greeting the guests at the front door and taking them to the dining room. Mr Carter was there to serve them. They were all talking together very quietly when Mrs Brompton and Miss Catherine walked in. It went very quiet but as Mrs Brompton walked around the room talking to people, the noise got a bit louder as everyone relaxed. William had gone downstairs to show the villagers into the servants dining room where the noise was a lot louder. Betty was in the upstairs dining room serving and Wyn was downstairs. Wyn was having more trouble with the downstairs guests than Betty was with her upstairs ones and she was feeling extremely tired. They were keeping her running around serving them. It was very late before the last funeral guest had left and both Wyn and Betty felt absolutely drained. As they had managed to get something to eat during the long day, all they wanted to do was go to bed but Mrs Davis made them sit down and have a cup of tea first, then told them to go up and sleep. When they got up to their room they both quickly stripped off their clothes and jumped straight into bed as the room was extremely cold. They snuggled up together for warmth and started touching each other's bodies until they both cried out in pleasure and then fell into a satisfied sleep.

The next day there was a commotion coming from the stables and Ned came running up to the house.

'Nero has gone,' he shouted, 'his stable is empty. He can't be far away because I have only just mucked him out, he was there then. I only went to get fresh hay and when I got back he was gone.'

All the available staff ran back to the stables with him. Wyn, Betty and William were amongst them. They spread out to see if they could find anything.

'Let's go back to the barn,' suggested Wyn. 'You never know, he could have been taken there.'

Betty and William agreed.

We'll all go together,' said William, 'if there is someone there he could be dangerous.'

They crept up to the barn door and looked through a crack in the wall. They could see a horse's tail so knew Nero was in there.

'Go and get Ned,' William whispered to Betty.

Betty ran off.

'Keep quiet,' William said very quietly, 'we can't do anything until Ned gets here. Just stay out of sight.'

Luckily there was no movement inside or outside the barn. Ned and Betty came running back. Ned had a shotgun with him so he and William pushed open the barn door. Inside they could see Nero but there was no sign of anyone else.

'What now?' asked William.

'We wait,' replied Ned.

William called to Wyn and told her and Betty to go and see if they could find Constable Wilson. They ran back to the house where Constable Wilson was sitting in the kitchen having a cup of tea.

'Come quick,' Wyn said, 'they've found Nero but there is no sign of anyone else.'

When they got back to the stables they found William and Ned inside. William was sitting on top of a man.

'This man is employed by Sir John Porchester,' William told Constable Wilson, 'his name is Pratt.'

'Let him up,' the Constable told William, 'I want to talk to him.'

William let Pratt up and Constable Wilson sat him down on a hay bale.

'Alright, why did you steal the horse?'

Pratt looked up and told the Constable that Sir John Porchester had instructed him to steal the horse because Charles Brompton owed him a lot of money through gambling and he wanted some of it back now, he didn't want to wait to maybe get some of it out of Mr Brompton's Estate. There would be a lot of creditors. Nero was a Thoroughbred and was worth a lot of money.

Constable Wilson took him up to the house to see Mrs Brompton, 'she will have to decide what to do,' he said. When they got up to the house William took them into the hall and told them to wait there until he had spoken to Mr Carter. He went up to Mr Carter's room and told him what had been going on. Mr Carter said he would have to speak to Mrs Brompton.

'Wait downstairs with them,' he told him. 'I'll be down in a moment.'

William went back downstairs and told the others they just had to wait. A few minutes later Mr Carter came down and told them that Mrs Brompton would see them.

'You are to go too,' he told William and Ned.

They all went up to the drawing room where Mrs Brompton was waiting. She asked a lot of questions and then said that Pratt could take Nero but Sir John Porchester had to agree to wipe out the rest of the debt in return. The horse would not leave the stables until he had agreed. Constable Wilson told her that this was agreeable to him but first he wanted to question Pratt about the murder of Mr Brompton to make sure he wasn't involved.

'Murder,' Pratt exclaimed, 'I wasn't involved in no murder, I just did what I was told and nicked the horse.'

'Well, you won't mind coming with me so that I can make my own mind up about that.'

He turned and nodded to Mrs Brompton, took hold of Pratt's arm then left. William and Ned went downstairs to the kitchen and told Wyn and Betty what had happened.

'What do you think?' Wyn asked them, 'do you think it was him that killed Mr Charles?' 'No,' said Ned, 'I think he was just after the horse. I'd better get back to the stables and settle Nero, he'll be very upset after all this.'

The next day Constable Wilson came into the kitchen and told them that he had let Pratt go because he didn't think it was him that killed Mr Charles.

'It wasn't him that had the camp site in the trees,' he told them, 'we never did find out who that was, they never came back. We were there for a couple of days but nothing. He says he was still in London when Mr Charles was killed, Sir John Porchester had a house party so all the staff were needed.'

'Do you believe him?' William asked.

'Yes, I think so,' replied Constable Wilson. 'I should be hearing back from Huddersfield soon about Frank Cooper's family so we might have more clues to go on.'

CHAPTER EIGHT

A few days later Wyn was cleaning the bedrooms when she heard a scream come from the direction of the stables. She ran downstairs and out of the front door, William was already outside.

'Did you hear that?' Wyn asked him.

'Yes, where was it coming from?' he asked.

'From the stables I think,' replied Wyn.

They ran towards the stables and got there in time to see Ned backing slowly away from the door.

'What's going on?' asked William.

Ned didn't say anything, just pointed. William turned and looked, 'oh my god!' he exclaimed. Inside William saw Miss Catherine sitting on a bale of hay with the Frank Cooper lookalike standing behind her holding a knife to her throat. They could hear him saying, 'I can see what Frank saw in you, you feel and smell so good.' He moved his free arm down her body and started stroking her breasts. 'Maybe I'll have a taste of your body before I kill you.' He suddenly saw William and Ned watching him. 'Don't come near or I'll kill her,' he told them.

'You aren't Frank,' said William, 'I cut him down so who are you?'

'He's George Cooper, Frank's identical twin brother,' a voice behind him said.

William turned round to find Constable Wilson standing behind him. 'We've just heard from the Constable in Huddersfield. George here disappeared not long after Frank died. He's been camping out around here since then looking for an opportunity to get back at the Brompton's.'

'Yeah,' George cut in, 'I was going to kill them all for what they did.'
Catherine Brompton was in tears by now, 'I loved Frank,' she sobbed.
'Maybe you did,' George replied, 'but you didn't stop him being sacked and sent away did you?'
'I wasn't here, I was sent to a school abroad straight away,' she cried, 'I didn't know what had happened to him.'
George started edging her out of the door. 'Stay back,' he warned them, 'don't try anything, she'll die if you do.'
He pushed Catherine out of the door and backed her away from the stables.
'Don't follow us' he warned.
Wyn had been out of sight the whole time this had been going on but had heard everything. As George was backing Catherine out of the door she ducked out of sight behind the stables. She watched as George pushed Catherine across the field. Wyn ran alongside them on the other side of the hedge that ran along the edge of the field, she could see that Catherine was crying and trying to talk to George. Wyn followed them until they entered a small shed on the far edge of the estate, she watched them go in then ran back to the house. She ran up to William, Ned and Betty breathing heavily. Once she caught her breath she told him where they were.
'Constable Wilson has gone back to the station to get more men,' William told her. 'We'll have to go and get him ourselves.'
The light was beginning to fail by the time they made their way towards the shed that Wyn had seen them enter. When they got there they could see a faint light shining in the

window. They crept over and looked through. George was sitting on a bed with Catherine. He had his arm around her. They couldn't hear what he was saying but they could see him stroking her face gently with his fingers. Catherine put her hand around his head and brought his face down to hers. She kissed him long and hard.

'Oh no!' exclaimed Wyn, 'she's pretending he's Frank.'
George was caressing her breasts and running his hands all over her body. Catherine pulled the pins out of her hair and ran her hands threw it seductively. She undid her dress and George helped her take it off until she was just dressed in her under clothes. George quickly took his clothes off and Catherine lay down on the floor waiting for him. He started kissing her all over and they saw her body arch in pleasure. George suddenly ripped her underwear off, lay on top of her and thrust his hard member into her.

'Come on, now's our chance,' said William, 'let's get Catherine away from him.'

They pushed the door open and rushed in. William pulled George up off of Catherine and Ned hit him hard. He went down and Ned hit him again just to make sure then tied him up with the rope William had found in the shed.

Catherine was crying and screaming, 'leave Frank alone, I love him.'

'It's not Frank,' Wyn told her.

'It really isn't,' added Betty, 'we saw his dead body. We know it's not him.'

Catherine just broke down completely and Wyn and Betty had to support her all the way back to the house where Mrs Danvers took her off them and led her upstairs to her bedroom. William and Ned put George into a wagon and took him into the village to find Constable Wilson.

'How did you get him?' he asked.

'It was Wyn who found him,' William told him. 'She followed them and then came and got us.'

'What will happen to him now?' asked Ned.

'He'll go to prison for a very long time,' replied the Constable. 'There's no doubt it was him who killed Charles Brompton.'

The next day Mrs Danvers came down to the kitchen and told them that Mrs Brompton had decided that she'd had enough of the bad luck they'd had since they'd been at the country house and she had to see the family solicitor to sort things out, so they were all going back to London. Wyn and Betty were to start packing up the kitchen and William and Ned were to pack up the rest of the house.

'What's going to happen to Ned?' Betty later asked Mrs Davis, 'there aren't any horses in London.'

'It looks like Mrs Brompton needs him for something else because he's coming with us,' Mrs Davis replied. Betty was relieved that she wouldn't have to say goodbye to Ned as she was getting very fond of him.

'Think of all the places I can take him in London,' she remarked to Wyn, 'he's never been there. We could all go out together it will be fun.'

The next few days were hectic with everything having to be packed up.

'It doesn't look like we are ever coming back,' commented Betty.

'We aren't,' replied Mrs Davis, 'Mr Carter says this house is going to be sold to pay off Mr Charles's debts.'

'That's a shame,' said Wyn, 'I've enjoyed it here.'
'Me too,' replied Betty, 'this was my first time in the country and I really liked it but it'll be nice to get back to smoky, noisy old London.'
On the last night Wyn, Betty, William and Ned walked down to the village inn for the last time. They had a few glasses of ale and then walked slowly back to the house.
'I'm going to miss this,' William remarked.
'Me too,' replied Wyn, 'even though some awful things have happened.'
When they got back to the house, Ned took Betty off one way and William took hold of Wyn's hand and pulled her towards one of the outbuildings near the house.
'It's too dark,' exclaimed Wyn.
'Just wait here,' William told her. He disappeared inside and Wynn saw a faint light appear. 'Come in,' William said. Wyn walked through the door to find a bed of hay with a blanket laid over it and a lit oil lantern hanging from a hook.
'Oh my,' she exclaimed, 'you've been busy.'
William came over to her and put his arm around her.
'I just wanted our last night here to be special,' he told her. He pulled her closer to him and kissed her gently on the mouth.
'It's lovely,' Wyn told him as she kissed him back. The kiss between them grew more passionate and she could feel the hardness of him against her. They sank down on to the hay bed he had made. She pushed herself against him and he moaned. She let her hand wander down his body until she could feel his erect member. She took hold of him through his clothes and started moving her hand up and

down. He was kissing her harder, pushing his tongue in her mouth, it was making her feel very excited. He started undoing her blouse which made her pause and push him away.

'No,' she said, 'we can't, I don't want a baby.'

'It's alright,' William replied, 'there are other things we can do.'

His hand skimmed over her erect nipples and she moaned. She opened his trousers and pulled his erect manhood out. She started moving her hand up and down along the length of him. He was really moaning by now. 'Oh don't stop,' he said. While she carried on moving her hand, she guided his hand further down her body until he reached the heart of her sex. Holding on to his finger she showed him how she liked to be touched. He started rubbing in her special place and she arched her back in pleasure. He was breathing heavier now, 'faster,' he said, 'do it faster. Ooh that's it don't stop, yes that's it,' he was saying while he was moving his finger round and round her intimate place. She could feel such a strong wave of pleasure building in her body, she didn't think she could stand it. William was writhing in pleasure now, 'oh that feels wonderful,' he was saying, 'don't stop, oh that's it,' and she felt him shudder as his seed spilled out over her hand. At that moment Wyn felt her body tense then her body seemed to explode in pleasure. She had never felt like this, not when she touched herself or when Betty touched her. This was something special.

When Wyn and Betty were in bed that night they talked about their experiences.

'I really love William,' Wyn told Betty.

'You didn't let him did you?' asked Betty.

'No,' Wyn told her, 'we just kissed and touched each other. It was the best feeling I've ever had. I want him so much.'

'I know, we're the same. I nearly gave in but I'm just too scared about what could happen.' said Betty.

Wyn sighed and said, 'it's getting so hard to stop, I just want more of him. I want to feel his hardness inside me.'

'I know, but stay strong, you never know, you might get married,' Betty told her.

'Oh that would be good,' replied Wyn. 'Imagine being married to William. Sleeping with him every night with his hard body next to me in bed.' She shivered with pleasure. Betty laughed, 'go to sleep,' she told Wyn, 'we have a long journey tomorrow.'

CHAPTER NINE

The next day was freezing cold with a thick layer of snow on the ground.

'Oh my,' exclaimed Wyn, 'this is going to be a long and cold journey back to London.'

'It certainly is,' agreed Mrs Davis, 'you'll have to put all your warmest clothes on. Come on now, get moving, we have a lot of work to do before we leave even though most of the house has already been emptied. Run upstairs and help Miss Catherine and Mrs Brompton with their belongings.'

Wyn went along to Miss Catherine's room to find her just sitting despondently on her packing chest. 'Is this all your things?' Wyn asked her. Catherine nodded. 'Come along then,' Wyn said, 'we have to get this chest downstairs.' Catherine looked up at her, 'I don't want to go back to London, I don't want to be anywhere where Mother is. She has ruined my life,' she said.

'You can't stay here,' Wyn told her, 'the house is going to be sold. Come on. I'll help you get the chest down the stairs.' Wyn took her arm and led her down to where Mrs Brompton was waiting for them.

'Come on, Catherine' she said, 'we need to leave for the village, we have to say goodbye to some people.'

'No,' replied Catherine, 'I'm not going, I don't want to be with you.'

'You will do what I tell you,' Mrs Brompton replied angrily, 'you have caused enough trouble for this family already. It's because of you I've lost my husband and now have to sell this house, so stop being troublesome and do as you are told. When we get to London you're not staying there, you will be going to live with your Aunt Constance in Surrey.'

Catherine didn't respond, she just sighed, gave her mother a frosty look and walked out of the door. Mrs Brompton followed her then turned and told Wyn that they would be gone for a couple of hours and that they would be leaving for the station at midday so they all had to be ready to leave. Wyn went down to the kitchen and told Mrs Davis what Mrs Brompton had said.

'That only gives us a couple of hours,' Mrs Davis said, 'you two girls run up to your room, bring down your boxes then go and find William and Ned. Tell them to search the house and the stables to make sure there is nothing left behind. Then they can go and tell the carriage drivers what time to be here.'

Mr Carter had organised local men to drive the carriages to take everyone to the station before he and Mrs Danvers had left for London to get the London house organised for the family's return.

Just before midday Mrs Brompton and Catherine came back from the village, the carriages had already arrived and were being loaded with all the chests. Wyn and Betty were already sitting in the second carriage ready to leave. William helped Mrs Brompton and Catherine up into the first carriage then jumped in with them. Mrs Davis and Ned climbed into the carriage with Wyn and Betty. They all looked at the house for the last time as the carriages started moving. Wyn sighed and commented, 'I'm going to miss it here.'

'Me too,' replied Betty. They looked at the passing scenery. 'Doesn't it look different in the snow,' remarked

Betty as they passed the village they had spent some fun times in.

'Yes,' Wyn agreed. 'You can hardly recognise it. How strange it looks with no-one around.'

When they finally reached the station they felt a bit battered and bruised after being thrown about for what seemed like hours. 'Oh my,' exclaimed Betty, 'that hurt in all the wrong places.'

'I know what you mean,' replied Wyn, 'I'm sure I've got a bruised bottom.'

They got all the chests off the carriages and then walked into the station. They sat down on the cold benches to wait for the train to arrive.

'It's late,' Mrs Brompton complained. She and Catherine went into the waiting room which had better and more comfortable seating. They had only been waiting for about ten minutes when the train arrived.

'Thank God for that,' muttered Betty, 'I'm freezing.'

All the chests were put into the baggage carriage and everyone clambered into first class. Mrs Brompton had told them that they would all be travelling first class in case she needed them for anything during the journey. A corridor ran all along one side of the train so moving from carriage to carriage was easy. It was strange for her to be travelling alone and she wanted to make sure she had help if she needed it. Wyn climbed in and looked around the carriage.

'This is very grand,' she remarked.

'Yes,' agreed Betty, 'I could get used to this.'

The carriage had very comfortable upholstered seats but was very cold although Mrs Brompton had purchased foot

warmers for everyone which helped them keep a bit warmer. The train started moving with a jolt that knocked Betty off her feet. She landed on the seat in a heap with her skirt up around her waist. The others in the carriage burst out laughing as she sat up red faced and straightened her skirt. 'Shut up you lot,' she exclaimed. 'It's not funny.'
'It is where we're sitting,' laughed Wyn.
They settled down and watched the passing scenery with interest. The train went through several tunnels which made Betty give a small scream as it took her by surprise when the carriage suddenly went dark. Wyn jumped when she felt a hand touch her breast until she realised that it was William making good use of the darkness of the tunnel. After they had been travelling for about two hours, Mrs Brompton looked in through the door and told them to go to the restaurant car to get some lunch.
'I don't want to sit in there by myself,' she told them. 'Catherine refuses to come with me so I would be very happy if you all would join me.'
They all stood up and followed her willingly along the corridor until they entered the restaurant car. It had plush purple upholstered seats and there were vases of flowers on each table. When Mrs Brompton had been seated at one of the tables she asked Mrs Davis to sit with her as she didn't want to dine alone. Wyn, Betty, William and Ned were then shown to another table. There was no choice of food but none of them cared what they ate, it was something they had never had the opportunity of doing before and they were determined to make the most of it. After they had all eaten they went happily back to their carriage.

William and Ned then promptly fell asleep. Wyn looked over at them.

'Typical,' she remarked.

They were travelling through sparsely populated countryside with few stations. They entered a very long tunnel and Wyn felt William sit down next to her. He turned her face towards him and gave her a long lingering kiss. 'Oh Wyn,' he whispered, 'I do want to be with you.' They suddenly came out of the tunnel and Wyn wasn't surprised to see Betty and Ned kissing passionately on the other seat. Wyn cleared her throat very loudly and Betty and Ned jumped apart. Betty's face went very red and she looked embarrassed. Wyn and William just grinned at each other and looked innocent. When they next looked out of the window they were going past a very large factory.

'What do you suppose they make in there?' asked Betty.

'I can see a sign on the side that says Huntley and Palmers Biscuit Factory. Looks like a grim place to work,' William said, 'I'm glad I don't work somewhere like that, it's alright working for Mrs Brompton.'

'I wouldn't like to work in a place like that neither,' agreed Wyn, 'I'm quite happy where I am.'

They were entering a more densely populated area so they knew they would soon be arriving at Waterloo Station. They were covered in a light film of soot by the time the train stopped and it gave them all a laugh. They found carriages waiting for them and were happy once they and all the baggage were on them.

When they finally arrived at the house they were all exhausted.

'What a journey,' remarked Wyn.

'Oh I don't know, it had its interesting bits,' William answered with a smile.

Mr Carter and Mrs Danvers were there to greet them. As William started taking Catherine and Mrs Brompton's chests up to their rooms, Mr Carter stopped him.

'Leave Miss Catherine's chest down here, her aunt will be here in the morning to take her to Surrey. She has to make do with any clothes left behind in her room.'

He turned to all of them, 'I know you are all very tired, but you're to take your things to your rooms and get changed into your uniforms. When you have done that you are all to gather in the drawing room as Mrs Brompton wants to talk to you.'

Wyn and Betty slowly walked upstairs to their room. When they opened the door it felt cold and smelt a bit musty.

'Urgh,' uttered Betty, 'we'll have to sort this room out. Come on quick put your things away and get changed, let's get out of here. Leave the door open when we leave, it might help get rid of the smell.'

They quickly got changed and made their way back down to the drawing room. Mrs Brompton was already there waiting for them. When everyone had gathered Mrs Brompton stood up to speak to them. She looked exhausted and had black smudges under her eyes.

'I know it has been a hard time for all of you over the last few weeks and I thank you for all the help you have given me. Things now have to change in my life so I just wanted you to know what is going to happen. The house in the country is going to be sold. I understand from the Estate Manager that there is someone already interested. There will only be a small staff kept on here. This will consist of Mrs Davis, William, Betty and Wyn. You will have no specific tasks but I hope the house will still run smoothly with just you four. I have brought Ned with us as I will no longer need a groom but, before we left for the country, Mr Brompton had bought a new motorcar and I would like Ned to learn how to drive it so he can become the new chauffeur.' She turned to Ned and asked, 'is that alright with you Ned?'

'Yes Mrs Brompton,' he replied, 'I'll be very happy to do that.'

Mrs Brompton smiled and said, 'on a lighter note, I have to tell you that Mr Carter and Mrs Danvers are getting married and will be leaving to go and work in a hotel in Kensington.'

'Oh how wonderful,' Mrs Davis exclaimed.

'Congratulations to both of you.'

'The wedding will be held here,' continued Mrs Brompton, 'and will be happening next week. Will you be able to arrange a wedding breakfast by then?' she asked Mrs Davis.

Mrs Davis looked at Betty and Wyn and both of them nodded. She then turned back to Mrs Brompton and said, 'yes, we'll get it done.'

'Good,' replied Mrs Brompton, 'I'll leave it in your hands. Mrs Danvers will tell you exactly when and what kind of things she wants.'

She looked at Ned and told him that the car was in the newly built garage at the back of the house. 'There is a room above the garage for you to sleep in and another for your ablutions. After you have had something to eat, go down there and get some sleep, you can have a look at the car in the morning and see if you can figure out how to drive it. There is extra land next to the garage, so just have a go there.'

She turned back to the rest of them, 'as we knew you all would be exhausted after travelling, Mrs Danvers has done a small buffet for you in the kitchen. I would like a tray of food to be brought up to mine and Catherine's rooms. Catherine will be leaving in the morning to stay with her aunt in Surrey.' She gave them all a tired smile and left the room.

They slowly walked down to the kitchen where the table was covered in food. 'Oh my,' exclaimed Mrs Davis, 'this looks wonderful,' she turned and smiled at Mrs Danvers. 'On behalf of all of us, thank you,' she said.

Wyn's mouth was watering and she was suddenly starving. 'Well don't just look at it,' Mrs Danvers told them, 'go ahead and eat.'

They all sat down at the table and filled their plates. Mrs Danvers filled plates for Mrs Brompton and Cartherine then took them upstairs to their rooms. It was very quiet as they were all trying to take in the information they had been given. Wyn turned to Betty and asked her what she thought. 'Do you think we can keep this house going with just us'?

'I don't know,' replied Betty, 'we'll just have to be really organised. I suppose it will help that it is just Mrs Brompton here. She is not untidy like Catherine. I think we'll have to write down what to do in each room every day.'

'Be quiet and eat,' Mrs Davis told them, 'you'll have time to talk about everything tomorrow.'

After they had finished eating, Wyn and Betty cleared the table and washed up.

'Take a warming pan up to your room and go to bed now,' said Mrs Davis. 'Don't worry about being down here early in the morning. Have a bit of a rest. I think there is going to be special tasks for you to do.' When they got to their room it smelt less musty now but was still freezing cold.

'Quick, put the pan in the bed so it can warm it up a bit before we get in,' instructed Betty. They stripped their uniforms off and got into bed.

'Ooh it's so cold,' shivered Wyn.

'Come and snuggle up against me,' said Betty. Wyn snuggled up against Betty's back and could feel the warmth starting to spread up her body.

'Oh that's better,' she said. Suddenly Betty jumped, 'get your cold feet off me,'

'Sorry,' mumbled Wyn who was already half asleep. Betty smiled in affection and closed her own eyes.

CHAPTER TEN

The next morning Mrs Brompton's sister Abigail turned up to take Catherine home with her. She was a very stout woman with hair tightly pulled back into a bun and a naturally stern expression but she smiled kindly at Catherine when she came down the stairs.

'Don't look so worried' she told her. 'You are not going to a prison. We have a lot of parties planned. I know you are supposed to still be in mourning, but your mother and I have decided that you are too young to worry about that and you should be having some fun. You never know, you might meet a suitor. Your cousins have plenty of eligible friends.' She turned to William, 'can you take Miss Catherine's chests out to the carriage please,' she asked. She then turned back to Catherine and told her to say goodbye to her mother. Catherine walked up to her mother and kissed her on the cheek but didn't look at her. Mrs Brompton put her hand under her chin and lifted her face to look at her.

'Don't worry about anything, it's going to be alright,' she said, 'just have some fun and try to forget everything that's happened, it's all in the past.'

Catherine gave a little sob and hugged her mother tightly.

'Go along now,' Mrs Brompton said. 'I will come and see you soon.' She followed them out of the house to wave goodbye. When she came back in, she ran up the stairs sobbing. Mrs Danvers followed her up shaking her head sadly. Wyn, Betty, William and Ned walked slowly down to the kitchen.

'That was so sad,' exclaimed Wyn, 'I do feel sorry for Miss Catherine.'

'And Mrs Brompton,' Betty quickly added.
'Come on, we've got work to do,' said Ned.
While Ned went back down to the garage to see the new motor car, Wyn, Betty and William were told by Mr Carter that they were to go round the house looking for anything that may be of value to sell. 'Mrs Brompton needs all the money she can get hold of to pay off Mr Brompton's gambling debts. The sugar plantation isn't doing too well and she doesn't want to have to sell this house too. Look absolutely everywhere, your jobs here may depend on it,' he told them. 'It will take you a few days but take your time, don't miss anything.'
Just then the bell from the drawing room rang.
'I'll leave it in your hands,' he told them as he left the room to answer the bell.
'Let's start in the attics and work down the house,' suggested William.
They went up the stairs to the attics. Wyn and Betty's bedroom was up there too. 'I don't think we need to search in that room, Betty told him. 'There's nothing of value in there.' William looked at Wyn intently.
'Yes there is,' he replied. Wyn just blushed and didn't reply. Either side of their room were the attic rooms. There were no windows in there and it was very dark.
'I think we need a couple of lanterns, I'll go and get them,' said Betty.
'Alright but don't be long,' William told her. When Betty had gone William grabbed Wyn and kissed her passionately. 'Ooh I've missed this,' he groaned as he rubbed himself against her. Wyn moaned as she felt his hard erection push against her.

'When can we be together again?' he asked her.
'I don't know,' she replied, 'we've got a lot of work to do now but we must get some time off soon, I'll ask Mrs Davis and let you know.'
William jumped back as he heard Betty coming back.
'I've got them,' she said as she came up the last set of stairs. She was breathing hard, 'oh them stairs,' she moaned, 'give me a minute to get my breath back.' When she had recovered they went into the first room which was full of all kinds of stuff.
'How on earth are we going to look through this lot?' Wyn grumbled. 'There's loads of it.' There was old furniture, kitchen equipment and general rubbish. They did find a few paintings they thought may be of value so they put them to one side. Wyn came across an old wooden box and opened it. Inside were a lot of necklaces, bracelets and earrings that sparkled when the light hit them.
'Come and see this,' she told the others.
'Oh my,' exclaimed Betty, 'look at this lot.'
'What do you think?' Wyn asked William, 'do these look like they are valuable?'
'Oh yes,' replied William, 'they look like real stones, we'll let Mr Carter have a look. Come on, we'll do it now, it'll give us a break.'
They took the paintings they had found as well as the jewellery and went to find Mr Carter. 'Look what we've found,' they said. Mr Carter looked in the box and said, 'well done, this looks like it could be worth some money. Keep looking there may be more of it. Go and have a cup of tea first, you look like you need it.' When they got to

the kitchen they found Ned sitting at the table with a cup of tea. He was covered in oil and muck.

'How's it going?' William asked him.

'I've finally found how to start it,' Ned told him. 'It's pretty scary though. I'm going to try and drive it when I've finished my tea.'

'Do you know what kind of motor vehicle it is?' asked Betty.

'It's an Alldays & Onions Traveller,' Ned told them. 'It's brand new. There aren't many of them available. I don't know how Mr Brompton got hold of one.'

'He won it at cards, Mr Carter told me,' William told him. 'Mrs Brompton doesn't know, he told her he bought it.'

'That explains a lot,' said Ned. 'I wondered why he would have bought it. Oh well, better go and see if I can drive it.' Good luck they told him.

'Right come on,' William said, 'let's go back and see what else we can find. We'll try the other attic room.'

They walked back up the stairs to the top floor and tried to open the other attic room door. William pushed it but it wouldn't budge. He got Wyn and Betty to help him. They all pushed but it still wouldn't open. 'What can be stopping it do you think?' Betty asked him.

'I don't know,' replied William. 'Keep pushing, it has to give in the end.'

They kept really pushing the door and eventually it started moving. It took them another hour to get the door open fully.

'Grab the lanterns.' William told Wyn, 'let's have a look at what was holding the door.' They walked in with the lanterns to find a large safe had fallen against the door.

'This looks like it might hold something valuable,' remarked Betty as she tried to open it. 'It's locked,' she said.

'Look around, there may be a key somewhere here,' William told them. They moved everything around the safe but couldn't find the key. 'Keep looking,' William said, 'it's got to be here somewhere.' Betty was looking in a drawer of an old desk when she found a small bag. Looking inside she saw a large key.

'I think I've found it,' she said excitedly. She took it over to William who tried it in the keyhole. It was a bit stiff but eventually the door opened. Inside they found a bunch of share certificates.

'Put these outside the door,' he told Wyn, 'I think this is the sort of stuff Mrs Brompton wants.' They also found a bundle of what looked like legal documents. 'We better take these too,' said William. He looked inside again but as there was nothing else in there, he shut the door. As they went further into the room Betty suddenly gave a little scream,

'Urgh I've just walked through a huge cobweb,' she told them, 'hurry up I don't like spiders.' The only other things they found were a few more old paintings.

'We'll take these downstairs now, it's beginning to get dark and the lanterns are fading. I don't think there is anything else up here anyway,' he said. 'Come on I'm starving.'

He let Betty and then Wyn go out first, managing to squeeze Wyn's behind as she went in from of him. Wyn jumped but gave a little giggle.

'What's up?' Betty asked her.

'Nothing,' replied Wyn, 'just thought I felt something.'

Betty just looked at her and shuddered as she started picking bits of cobweb out of her hair.
When they got down to the kitchen Mrs Davis was stirring a big pot of stew on the stove. 'Good you've finished,' she said, 'go wash your hands and sit down at the table. William go down to the garage and call Ned, your supper is ready. '
Wyn and Betty walked into the scullery to wash their hands. William went out of the back door and walked down to the garage. He could hear an engine revving and a lot of swearing coming from inside. When he walked in he saw a very dirty and oily Ned kicking the tires of the car. He laughed at the sight and asked Ned what he was doing.
'This blooming car,' Ned shouted, 'I'm never going to get the hang of it. I can get it started and can even get it moving but how it works, I don't know and I've got to fix it if it goes wrong, so I have to know what makes it work.'
'I wouldn't worry about that until it does go wrong,' William told him, 'as long as you can make it move, I think that's enough for now. It's only been a day, don't be so hard on yourself. Anyway leave it for now, it's getting dark and supper's ready. Mrs Davis told me to come and get you.'
Ned threw the tool he had in his hand down, took off the new overalls that he had been given to wear, wiped his hands on a rag and followed William out of the door locking it as he left. When they got back to the kitchen Wyn and Betty looked round at them and laughed at the sight of Ned.

'Look at the mess you are in,' exclaimed Mrs Davis, 'you're not sitting down at this table in that state, go and clean yourself up.'

When Ned came back looking a lot cleaner Mrs Davis put large bowls of delicious smelling stew in front of each of them. There was also newly baked bread on the table. 'This is lovely,' they all told her as they started eating. There was silence for a while as they all ate until they were completely full. 'Ooh that was smashing,' Wyn said, 'thank you Mrs Davis.'

'I hope you've left room for apple pie,' Mrs Davis said. 'There's some custard to go with it. Do you all want some?' 'Oh yes please,' they all responded. When they had finished eating Wyn and Betty carried their empty plates into the scullery and washed them and the pots and pans up. When they had finished and went back into the kitchen, Wyn made a big pot of tea for them all and they sat at the table and drank it chatting generally. It was getting quite late when the bell from the drawing room suddenly rang. William jumped up, I had better go and see what is wanted. He grabbed his jacket that was hanging from a coat rack, put it on and ran up the stairs. 'I wonder what Mrs Brompton wants at this time of night,' Wyn said. William was soon back down.

'I had to get Mrs Danvers,' he told them, 'Mrs Brompton was in a real state. There was something in that bundle of legal papers we found that shocked and upset her. I don't know what it was but she wants you, Ned, to take her in the motor car to see her solicitor tomorrow. Something is definitely up.'

Ned looked worried. 'It's the first time I've taken the car out on the highway,' he said, 'having Mrs Brompton in there with me is quite scary.'

'You'll be fine I'm sure,' William told him. 'She said to be outside the house at ten o'clock. You are to see Mr Carter before then so he can give you suitable clothes to wear.'

It was getting late so Mrs Davis told them all to get to bed as tomorrow was likely to be another busy day.

Wyn and Betty went up to their room. As Wyn reached up to take the pins out of her hair, Betty slipped her hands round her and started caressing her breasts. 'Ooh that feels nice,' Wyn said. She moved her own hands down her body until she came to the nub of her sex. She started moving her finger round and round and could feel the pleasure mounting. She turned round and kissed Betty hard, pushing her tongue into her mouth. Her hand then left her own body and she moved it down Betty's body until she reached the heart of her sex. Betty moaned as she touched her. 'Oh that's it,' she whispered as Wyn started moving her fingers around her. She felt Betty shudder as she moved her finger faster, 'don't stop,' said Betty, 'oh please don't stop.' Wyn felt Betty give one more shudder as she reached the peak of pleasure. 'Ooh,' she moaned, 'that was so nice. I like what we do so much. Lie down on the bed,' she told Wyn, 'I want to try something new.' Wyn lay down and Betty stripped off her clothes completely so she was naked. She started kissing Wyn all down her body stopping at her breasts. She took each nipple into her mouth and sucked hard. Wyn moaned. Betty then started kissing further down her body until she came to her sex. She tentatively put her tongue out and started licking. Wyn arched her back in total pleasure. 'Oh that's so good,' she said, 'I didn't know it could feel that nice.' Betty kept moving her tongue faster and harder. Wyn was writhing in pleasure now until her body suddenly went still and a wave of pleasure she had never felt before washed over her. When she had recovered slightly she told Betty it was the best ever. 'I'll have to do the same to you soon so that you know how nice it is,' she said. They snuggled up together and fell into a contented sleep.

CHAPTER ELEVEN

The next day Ned was outside in the car waiting for Mrs Brompton. Wyn caught a glimpse of him through the drawing room window. He was dressed very smartly in a grey jacket and trousers but looked very worried. She saw Mrs Brompton come out of the front door and get into the car. Ned had already started it so he just drove off very slowly. Wyn thought it looked like he was doing alright. She turned away from the window and went back to cleaning the drawing room. It was the first time she'd had to clean it by herself as Betty was doing the bedrooms. They had drawn up a rota for which rooms were to be done on what day by whom and it was working quite well. The house was still clean and tidy even though there was less staff. William was being taught how to do more duties by Mr Carter. Even Mrs Davis had more things to do than just cooking. She was to be a ladies maid if Mrs Brompton ever needed one and Mrs Danvers was showing her what to do. There wasn't much time left until Mr Carter and Mrs Danvers got married and Mrs Davis was trying to organise the food and had started the wedding cake, she needed Wyn and Betty's help so there wasn't a lot of time off for anyone yet. They were getting married in a small church near the house in a weeks time. Mrs Brompton was letting them have the wedding breakfast in the drawing room before they left for a honeymoon in Brighton. They would then be starting their new lives in the hotel they would be working at in Kensington. The wedding would be the last time the staff would see them.

It was lunch time when Ned got back. After dropping Mrs Brompton off at the front door, he put the car away and then came back to the kitchen. When Wyn, Betty and William came in for lunch he was already sitting at the table waiting for them. Once they had all settled down, he said 'you will never believe where we've been.'

'Where?' they all asked him, even Mrs Davis who didn't normally listen to gossip.

'I drove Mrs Brompton to the solicitor first, she was in there for quite a while. I assumed she was looking at Mr Brompton's Will when she came running out of there quite distressed, but she told me to drive to an apartment block in Chelsea. When we got there she asked me to go with her up to an apartment. She seemed very, very angry at something. She knocked on the door and a very attractive woman answered it. She was quite young with long blonde hair which was hanging loose. She was dressed in the height of fashion and had a very slender figure. Mrs Brompton said something very quietly to her that I couldn't hear but it made her go white and she invited us in. The apartment was large and was very tastefully furnished. There was a painting of her with Mr Charles on the wall above the fireplace.' As he told them this they all sighed knowingly. Ned continued, 'Mrs Brompton spotted it and started shouting at the woman. Her name turned out to be Lillian and she had been Mr Charles's mistress for three years. Mrs Brompton told her that Mr Charles was dead and she collapsed on the floor in tears. She was sobbing that she really loved him and she thought he loved her. Mrs Brompton told her she didn't think so, he only ever loved himself and gambling. Mrs Brompton ended up feeling sorry for her and told her that she would have to leave the apartment but she would give her one month to do it. She would even make sure she had some money so that she could find somewhere else to live but it wouldn't be as expensive as this apartment'.

'So that's what was in the bundle of legal documents,' William said. 'There must have been deeds to the apartment in there. That's how Mrs Brompton found her.'

'That's not all' Ned told them. 'We're going to another apartment block tomorrow.'

'Oh my' exclaimed Wyn,' how many mistresses did he have?'

'We'll soon find out,' replied Ned.

After lunch Ned went back to the garage to clean the car while Wyn and Betty helped Mrs Davis with the food for the wedding on Saturday. She was icing the wedding cake when Mrs Danvers walked in.

'Oh that looks lovely,' she exclaimed.

'You're not supposed to see it yet' she was told, 'it's meant to be a surprise.'

'What else are you doing'? Mrs Danvers asked her.

'Just wait and see' was the reply.

'Now get out of the kitchen so I can get on'

Mrs Danvers did as she was told and left smiling. Wyn came out of the scullery with a basket of iced roses.

'That was lucky,' she told Mrs Davis,' just as well I heard her so at least she didn't see these.' The cake was going to be covered in white icing with iced roses of pink, red and yellow set around it plus figures of the bride and groom in the middle.

'This is going to look wonderful' Wyn told Mrs Davis.

'I hope so,' was the reply. 'Now go and help Betty with the pies.'

Before Wyn went to join Betty in the scullery she asked Mrs Davis if she thought Mrs Danvers's brother was likely to be at the wedding.

'I don't know' replied Mrs Davis, 'why are you so interested in him'?

'He's the priest from our church in Wales' Wyn replied. 'He might have some news of my family so I hope he is.'

'Well I expect he will be,' Mrs Davis told her, 'he is her brother after all.'

The next day Ned took Mrs Brompton out in the car again. This time they went to an apartment block in Fulham. Wyn, Betty and William were waiting for him again at lunch time.

'Well?' they asked, 'what happened this time?'

'We went to the apartment' Ned told them 'but it was empty. The key had been given to the Concierge of the flats yesterday evening. I think Lillian, who we saw yesterday must have known this mistress and warned her. We were given a description of her and she sounds just like Lillian. Mr Charles must have a liking for young blonde women. There was nothing left in there, it had been stripped of everything. I think Mrs Brompton is going to sell the apartment in Fulham but she is going to give the other one to Miss Catherine to live in either on her eighteenth birthday or if she marries.'

'I wonder if that's the last one pondered Wyn.'

'It's the last one of the Deeds anyway,' replied Ned. 'One thing's for sure, all this is helping Mrs Brompton get over Mr Charles's death. She's even talking about not wearing mourning clothes anymore.'

'No-one could blame her,' said Wyn, 'why would any wife mourn for a man like him.'

'Come on you lot, stop gossiping,' Mrs Davis put in, you all have work to do. As the food is almost ready, Wyn and Betty you go and give the drawing room a good clean ready for the wedding, and remember all of you, there's still the basement to search.'

'How could I forget?' muttered Betty, 'all those spiders that are going to be down there, urgh.'

'We're going down there after the wedding,' William told her.

'Well, as you have all worked so hard for so long Mrs Brompton has said that you all can have time off after the wedding until Monday so you'll have Saturday afternoon and all of Sunday to do whatever you want.'

'That's great they all shouted!'

'We can go out somewhere all four of us,' said Wyn.

'We could go to the music hall on Saturday afternoon,' said Betty

'And a nice riverside pub on Sunday' Ned put in.

It was Mrs Danvers and Mr Carter's wedding day. The weather was cold but dry which they were thankful for as they had to walk to the Church. As Mrs Danvers was a widow who was remarrying, she was wearing a salmon satin gown trimmed with ostrich feathers. She had no bridesmaids or attendants. She wore a diamond necklace and carried a simple bunch of lilies. As she came down the stairs she was greeted by the rest of the household.

'You look beautiful,' Mrs Brompton told her.

Mr Carter was standing at the bottom of the stairs waiting for her. He was wearing a frock coat along with a double-breasted light grey waistcoat, dark grey tie and grey striped cashmere trousers.

'You look very nice too,' he was told.

They all felt very happy as they walked out of the house behind the bride and groom because they were all dressed in their Sunday best and they weren't working for a couple of days. Wyn took William's arm and Betty took Ned's as they walked. The church was full of flowers and looked lovely. Wyn kept looking around her to see if Father John was there but was very disappointed as she couldn't see him. After what seemed like a very quick service, it was all over and they were outside. They all had rice which they threw at the bride and groom who were laughingly trying to duck out of the way. Then they walked back to the house for the wedding breakfast. When she saw the cake Mrs Davis had lovingly prepared for them, the now Mrs Emily Carter was overcome. She thanked Mrs Davis with tears in her eye.

'I'm so grateful to all of you,' she said. 'I wish my brother had been here to see me married but he's not been very well, although I'm glad to say he's getting better now'

Mr Carter joined her and put his arm around his new wife.

'I too would like to thank all of you for your help in making this a very special day but I'm afraid I have to steal my wife away now so that we can catch our honeymoon train.'

Everyone moved down to the front door where there was a carriage waiting for them. It had been decorated with flowers and Mrs Carter nearly jumped for joy when she saw it. As they were about to get in Mrs Brompton did something employers didn't normally do, she hugged both of them. They both looked a bit shocked but pleased. Mrs Carter had a faint blush of pink in her cheeks.

'Have a good honeymoon,' Mrs Brompton told them 'and I hope you will be very happy in your marriage.'

'Thank you' Mrs Carter whispered tearfully.

They both got in the carriage and it moved off with everyone waving and shouting goodbye, be happy.

CHAPTER TWELVE

After the dishes from the wedding breakfast had been cleared away and washed up and the drawing room put back to its usual state, Wyn, Betty, William and Ned were free to do whatever they wanted to. As they were already dressed in their Sunday best, they just left the house straight away. It was a very cold but clear evening.

'Where shall we go'? Wyn asked,' it'll have to be indoors, it's too cold to go for a walk.'

'Let's go to the West End, we could find a music hall' replied William.

'I've never been to a music hall before,' said Wyn,

'Me neither' Ned put in, 'I'd like that.'

'Come on then,' William told them, 'we could get a drink as well as see the show, it'll be fun'.

They got a trolley bus into the West End which was packed with people. Everyone seemed very happy and out for a good time. They found the entrance to the music hall which was covered with huge posters and adorned with plaster statues with coloured lamps, the walls were lined with tarnished looking-glass and gilded trellis-work. They walked in and paid their money. Inside it was old, gaudy and crimson with a lot of gilding. Wyn and Ned were fascinated and couldn't stop looking at everything. There were little family parties that consisted of a father, mother and even a child or two sitting in the stalls. They looked like they were regular visitors as they all seemed to know one another, shaking hands and smiling at each other. There were several couples and a few older ladies, while the rest of the audience were made up of young clerks, who

were wearing a cigar behind their ears which was the fashion at that time. This made Wyn and Betty laugh.
'It just makes them look silly,' commented Wyn.
There were large ham sandwiches being handed round by cooks in white blouses, and glasses of port were being drunk by everyone. William and Ned got glasses for them all. There was a chairman sitting at a table in front of the orchestra who announced the next act and then sat back down and applauded himself with a little auctioneer's hammer. The performance started and after a song and a performance by a group of acrobats, came an odd exhibition by a young lady showing different swimming strokes in a large glass tank filled with water that Wyn thought was very strange. After that there was a lady singer who sang very loudly. There were also performing animals, strong-men, a magician and a ventriloquist. It was loud, mad and fun.
By the time they came out of the music hall they were all quite tipsy and happy. 'That was great,' Wyn said as she and Betty skipped down the road arm in arm.
'Hey wait for us,' shouted William and Ned running to catch up with them.
'We better get back to the house,' Betty said, 'it's getting a bit late.'
'Come on run, there's a trolley bus coming,' William told them. They all started running and managed to jump on.
'Ooh it's a cold night,' complained Betty snuggling up to Ned.
There was no response from Wyn or William as they only had eyes for each other and were oblivious to anyone else.

When they got back to the house Ned kissed Betty goodnight as he had to go back to the garage. He was trying his best to get Betty to go back with him but was having no luck. 'Goodnight Ned,' she said firmly, 'thank you for a very nice night.'

She, Wyn & William walked into the house through the kitchen door. Ned just shrugged, shouted goodnight and walked down to the garage. Wyn, Betty and William were surprised to see Mrs Davis was still up.
'Sit down and have a cup of tea,' she told them.
'Oh, I need this,' said Betty, 'it's freezing out there.'
When they had finished drinking their tea Mrs Davis turned to them and told them that Mrs Brompton had decided that, as Mr and Mrs Carter had left and there were no other staff in the house now, she wanted William to move to Mr Carter's room which was bigger than the one he was in and Wyn and Betty were to have a room each on the servants floor which would get them out of the cold and damp attic room. They could move their belongings in the morning but they could make up the beds in the rooms now and put warming pans in to warm them up.
'Oh my,' exclaimed Wyn, 'I've never had a room of my own.'
'Well, now you've finished your tea, go up and decide which room you want. William, you can move into your new room tomorrow. Goodnight to all of you, I'll see you bright and early in the morning.'
Once she had left the room, William went up to his new room and Wyn took the cups and saucers into the scullery and washed them up. She and Betty then left the kitchen and walked upstairs to see their new rooms. They both

walked into the first room, which was very nicely decorated.

'This is very nice,' commented Betty.

Then they went into the room next door which was also decorated nicely.

'I'll have this one,' said Wyn,

'Alright,' Betty agreed,' there's not much to choose between them really. There're both very nice. It's going to be strange not having you snuggled up against me. I'll miss you and our intimate times.'

'I know,' replied Wyn, 'I'm going to miss being with you too. We can still have our special conversations while we work though.'

'I know,' Betty agreed 'but it won't be the same.'

They gave each other a hug goodnight and went into their respective rooms.

When they had finished their normal duties the next day, they were all called to the drawing room by Mrs Brompton. 'I just wanted to let you know how things are,' she told them. 'Now there is so few of us living here, we are more like a family than mistress and servants so I wanted you to know everything. The country house has now been sold and the money I received for it is enough to pay off Mr Brompton's large debts. The shares he had were also worth a considerable amount of money. I now have enough to keep this house going so it won't have to be sold. I am also keeping the sugar plantation in Jamaica because, although it isn't doing too well, at least it gives some revenue. I have appointed a new manager for it so hopefully it will start doing better. Apparently he is a married man with two

children and comes highly recommended. His name is
Henry Williams.'

Hearing that name made Wyn look up and ask Mrs
Brompton if she knew where he was from.

'I understand he was from your neck of the woods, Wales',
was the response.

Wyn thought no, it couldn't be, it's just a coincidence,
there must be lots of Henry Williams from Wales.

'Do you think you might know him?' asked Mrs Brompton.

'My half-brother's name is Henry Williams,' Wyn told her
'but it's such a common name in Wales, I doubt if it's him.'

'I'll see if I can find out next time I write to him,' promised
Mrs Brompton. She then told Wyn, Betty and William to
start the search of the basement to see what was down
there. 'Although there is enough money so that all the
debts can be paid now,' she said,' it would be nice to know
what is down there. I have never been down there, have
any of you?'

They all told her they hadn't.

'Well, let me know what you find,' she said as she turned
to leave the room, 'and I would like to thank you all for
your help'.

Once they had been to the kitchen to collect lanterns, Wyn
told William to go down the basement steps first. 'You can
get rid of all the cobwebs,' she told him.

It was dark walking down the steps even with the lanterns.
The basement was very large and felt cold and damp. There
wasn't much down there, just a lot of old rugs and
furniture. William went further in and found a large
cupboard resting against the far wall.

'Come and look at this,' he told Wyn and Betty.

It was very ornate with intricate carving all over it. There was a small chest sitting next to it with the same carving all over it.

'I think these are from China,' William suggested, 'I saw something like this in a magazine Mrs Brompton had.'

'Look inside,' Wyn told him, 'there might be something valuable in there.'

William opened the door but there was nothing inside, it didn't even have a back to it.

'This is very strange,' William remarked, 'there seems to be some sort of door behind it, help me move it out of the way.'

They moved the cupboard to find a large door,' it's locked,' William told them after he tried to open it. 'We need to find a key.' He turned to Betty and asked her to go upstairs and have a look around Mr Brompton's study to look for it. 'Look in the desk under the window, I think I saw an elaborate key in there which looked something like the one that would open this door. I wondered what it would open. We'll stay here and search through the chest.'

After Betty had taken a lantern and gone up the stairs, William put his arm around Wyn and kissed her. The kiss got more passionate as Wyn opened her mouth to let his tongue slip in. William undid part of her blouse as his finger rubbed her nipples making them harden, he kissed her neck then moved his mouth down to her breast taking a nipple between his lips then sucking hard on it. Wyn moaned and tried to stop him.

'Don't,' she said putting her clothes back in order, 'Betty will be back in a minute.'

'When can we be together again?' he groaned, 'I want to be close to you, it's not the same doing it to myself.'
She looked at him in wonder, 'I never thought of you touching yourself,' she said. 'I thought it was just us that did that. You'll have to show me how you do it next time we're alone.'
'Only if you show me what you do,' he told her.
She just blushed and didn't say anything. 'Oh my,' she thought, that sounds interesting. William moaned in lust at the thought. They heard movement at the top of the stairs so jumped apart and started looking through the chest. There were some lovely bits and pieces of jewellery in there that Wyn took out to give to Mrs Brompton.
'I've found it,' Betty shouted as she started walking down the stairs.
She gave the key to William who tried it in the door. It took a bit of effort but William eventually managed to unlock it. It was a thick and heavy metal door that took all three of them to pull open. Once it was open and they put a light near it, they saw that it wasn't a cupboard but another room that was very enclosed. As they walked in, they noticed a strange musty smell but thought nothing of it as no-one had been in there for a long time. There was no window but there were vents in the top of the wall that let some air in. There were shelves running along the walls with some silver objects on them. There were also some large paintings in very ornate frames resting against the walls.
'These look like they could be worth something,' remarked Wyn, 'they look very old.'

Betty found a small wooden chest on the floor. She opened it and gasped.

'Oh my,' she said, 'look at this.'

Inside it was full of old coins. 'Where would these have come from,' she wondered, 'it looks like a treasure chest.'

Wyn and William went over to have a look.

'Maybe Mrs Brompton will know,' William told them.

There was another level to the chest so they took the top level off to find a document underneath. William opened it to find it was an I.O.U from The Right Honourable Frederick Huxley-Chadwick for the sum of one hundred and fifty thousand pounds.

'It's lunch time,' Wyn told them, 'let's go up and take the chest to Mrs Brompton. She's going to find this very interesting. We can come back later and finish searching.'

When they got upstairs they went to find Mrs Brompton.

'We've found a couple of interesting things,' they told her. William handed her the wooden box.

'Take a look in here,' he told her.

Mrs Brompton looked inside and got quite excited.

'All these old coins, they look like they could be roman, I'll have to find out where to take them, there must be somewhere that would be interested in them.'

'That's not all,' William told her,' look at the level underneath.'

Mrs Brompton took the top layer off and looked at the document underneath.

'Now that is something,' she exclaimed, 'it must be a gambling debt, I can do something with this.'

'I wonder what she means,' Wyn thought,' she obviously has something in mind. Oh well I suppose we'll find out sooner or later.'

'Did you find anything else down there?' Mrs Brompton asked.

'We did find some more paintings that look very old and some items of silver. Oh and I found some more items of very pretty jewellery,' Wyn replied.

'Apart from that, there is just some old furniture but we haven't finished yet,' William said. 'We found the old wooden chest in a room down there that had a metal door. There's a bit more in there to look at, we thought we'd go back down after lunch.'

'Let me know when you're ready,' Mrs Brompton said, 'I'd like to come down and see this room myself.'

When they had finished lunch William went upstairs to tell Mrs Brompton they were ready to go back down to the basement. Wyn and Betty were already down there when William and Mrs Brompton came down. William opened the door and they all walked in. Mrs Brompton looked around the room.

'I wonder how long this has been here?' she commented, 'my husband inherited this house from his parents so it could have been here a very long time.' She walked further into the room and picked up a very heavy silver vase.

'These things must have belonged to his family, she said. 'I've never seen them before.'

Wyn and Betty were moving the paintings resting on the wall at the back of the room when they saw an old rug rolled up in the corner.

'Look at this Wyn,' said to Mrs Brompton, 'how old do you think this is?'
'Very old from the look of it,' was the reply.
'Bring it out here so we can see it better.'
'Grab hold of the end,' Wyn told William, 'it's quite heavy.'
They carried it out of the room and laid it down on the basement floor. It was tied up in two places with old rope that had frayed in quite a few places.
'It's a good thing I thought to bring a knife down with me,' William said.
He cut the rope and then started unrolling the rug. The musty smell they had smelt in the room when they first walked in got stronger. They all looked at each other and William stopped unrolling.
'What do you think?' he asked them.
Mrs Brompton took deep breath and told him to carry on unrolling the rug. William carried on slowly and jumped back when a leg bone fell out.
'Stop unrolling now' Mrs Brompton told him. 'We are going to have to tell someone about this.' Wyn and Betty were looking at the bone in shock. 'Come on all of you upstairs now,' Mrs Brompton said. 'I'll lock the door and no-one is to come down here until the police have been informed.'
When they got upstairs Mrs Brompton sent William to the garage to tell Ned to drive to the nearest police station to report what had been found and then come back to the house to tell her what the police had said. When Ned got back he told them all that a couple of police constables would be coming round shortly to have a look at what they

had found. Until then no-one was to go anywhere near the basement. Mrs Brompton told them to have a cup of tea then carry on with their normal duties until the police arrived.

'They will need someone to show them where to go and they might need to talk to all of you even though you won't know anything. It must have been down there a long time,' she said. Wyn went into the scullery to start preparing vegetables for dinner while Betty went up to the bedrooms to start lighting the fires. It wasn't long before there was a knock on the door. William opened it to find two policemen standing outside.

'Come in he told them, I'll take you to where it is.'

He picked up a lantern and took them down to the basement. There were already a couple of lanterns down there and he lit them. The police constables went over to the rug and looked at the leg bone.

'Can you unroll the rug a bit more but very slowly they told him.'

William started unrolling the rug and more of the skeleton appeared. When he had finished unrolling he stood back. On the now completely unrolled rug lay a whole skeleton. William looked down at it in shock.

'I think we are going to have to inform Scotland Yard of this' the constable told him. 'It's too big for me to deal with. Come on out now, lock the door and give the key to me. We don't want anyone being tempted to come down here now.'

William took them up to see Mrs Brompton to let her know what they were doing and then went down to the kitchen to let the rest of the household know.

'Well I never exclaimed,' Mrs Davis, 'I wonder who the poor soul was.'

'They don't even know whether it was a man or a woman,' William told them 'or how long it's been down there. Mrs Brompton told them that the house had been in Mr Brompton's family for a long time,' said William, 'so it could have happened a long time ago.'

CHAPTER THIRTEEN

The next day Mrs Brompton called them together and told them that there would now be detectives investigating the body in the basement.

'In the meantime, she told them, 'I would like you to search through Mr Brompton's study thoroughly to find any papers you can about Mr Brompton's family. Any little thing could be of significance,' she said, 'so don't discount anything. The clue to who it was could be in there.'

They all felt quite excited about doing it as this was something completely different to their usual tasks. They went into the study which was very opulent. There was an enormous mahogany desk with a padded chair under the window with cabinets next to it and bookcases all around the walls.

'There must be hundreds of books in here,' said Wyn.

'Yes and we'll have to look through all of them,' replied William. 'You never know what might be hidden in one of them. This is going to take a long time.'

'I love it,' exclaimed Betty.'

'It's better than doing the cleaning or preparing vegetables,' put in Wyn.

'Come on stop chattering, let's get on with it,' William told them.

Wyn pulled a face at him but started looking in the cabinets.

'I don't really know what I'm looking for,' she muttered.

'Just take everything out and put it into a pile. Once we have emptied every drawer or cabinet in here, we'll have a look through it and anything interesting, we'll take to Mrs

Brompton and let her decide what's important,' replied William.

In the cabinet Wyn found all kinds of documents that were dated from the mid 1800's.

'There's some really old stuff in here,' she said as she started making a pile of papers.

Betty was looking through the drawers in the desk and found some old pictures.

'Look at these,' she told the others. 'I think these are of Mr Brompton when he was young but who's this boy?'

'I think there was an older brother,' William told her 'but I don't know what happened to him although I expect Mrs Brompton will probably know.'

Wyn was still looking through the cabinets and pulling things out of them. She came across some newspaper clippings from the Daily News about attacks on young women.

'What would these be doing in here?' she asked the others.

'That's very strange,' commented William,

'Yes, especially as there's a body in the basement,' added Wyn.

'Now don't let your imagination go wild,' William told her, 'it might just be a coincidence.' 'Hmm,' Wyn replied, 'we'll see.' She put the clippings on the growing pile of documents. 'Maybe Mrs Brompton can say something about this too.'

It was beginning to get dark so William told them to finish what they were doing, 'we'll start again in the morning,' he said. Wyn put the pile of documents on top of one of the cabinets and told Betty to do the same. The pile was quite big, it was going to take a while to go through them but

none of them minded. Once the study was tidy they all left and went downstairs to the kitchen. Mrs Davis looked up at them and started moaning about not having any help making dinner.
She said to Wyn, 'you can go and peel vegetables,'
'Betty, you go up and make up the table in the small dining room for Mrs Brompton. I know Mrs Brompton wants all of you to search for things, but I need help too so I want you to finish a bit earlier so that you can help me.'
'Alright,' they agreed.
When dinner was ready William was told to go and get Ned. He found him just sitting in the garage with the car looking very bored.
'I need something else to do,' he told William. 'Can't I come and help you?'
'I'll ask Mrs Brompton,' William told him. 'It might help keep Mrs Davis quiet.' William brought him up to date about everything that had happened so far.
'It sounds very interesting,' Ned said, 'I would really like to help. Life's certainly not boring with this family he added.'
After Wyn and Betty had finished their duties the next day they were all back in the study. Ned was with them this time as Mrs Brompton had agreed he could help too as there was nothing for him to do with the car. Wyn finished emptying the cabinets and then started looking through the hundreds of books on the shelves. Betty was still looking through the desk drawers and came across a Birth Certificate for Charles Brompton and one with the name George Edward Brompton on it.
'Who's he?' she asked.

'I don't know,' replied William, 'I've never heard that name. Put it on the pile for Mrs Brompton and forget about it for now.'

She finished clearing the desk drawers and then joined Wyn in looking through the books. Wyn came across an old family Bible that went back centuries. There was a complete list of all the Bromptons in the front.

'Here's that name again,' she told them. 'He was born in 1851 and Charles Prentice Brompton was born in 1853. It looks like he was the older brother.'

'This is strange,' William said, 'I've never heard that name mentioned. He's never visited the family since I've been here.'

'Maybe he died,' Wyn said.

'I suppose that could be it,' William agreed, 'you don't suppose the body in the basement could be him do you?' They all looked at each other and Wyn said 'no, surely not.'

'Just keep on searching,' William told them. 'There might be more about him in here somewhere.'

William was searching the top bookshelves when he found a large bundle of papers clipped together. 'I've found lists of the staff of the house from the beginning of 1800,' he told them. 'The family must have kept records of everyone. It could help in identifying whoever the body in the basement was if it wasn't George Brompton,' he added.

They were coming to the end of the search of everything apart from the books when Mrs Brompton came in. William showed her the pile of documents that she was going to have a look through. 'Oh my,' she exclaimed, 'this is going to take me a while.'

William showed her the Birth Certificate and the Bible that Wyn had found. She opened the Birth Certificate first and read the name and then she had a look at the first page of the Bible. 'It looks like I had a brother-in-law,' she said. 'I didn't know him. I'll have to try and find out who he is or was. Maybe the solicitor knows. I'll go and see him tomorrow.' She turned to Ned and told him to have the car at the front of the house at ten o'clock the next morning. She told the others that there would be two detectives from the Criminal Investigation Department coming to the house and that they were to give them any help they needed.

'In the meantime keep looking through the books,' she said, 'there may be some more interesting things inside them. Look more carefully now, I don't want you to miss anything.' She then turned and left the room. Wyn took a few books off the middle shelf and took them over to the desk. There was nothing in the first few books but in the last book there was a piece of paper that looked like a torn page of an accounts book.

'Look at this,' she said to William. 'It mentions that name again with some figures by the side of it.'

'Keep hold of that,' William told her, 'Mrs Brompton might find it interesting.'

Betty had taken more books from the middle shelf. She suddenly exclaimed, 'I've found some pages too. Why are they hidden in books do you think? Who is this man?'

'Just keep the pages together and keep looking,' William told them.

They cleared the middle shelf and had quite a pile now of the pages.

'Take them straight up to Mrs Brompton,' William told Wyn, 'she might need to take them with her tomorrow.' Wyn took them up to the drawing room where Mrs Brompton had started looking through the documents they had found so far.

'We thought you might need to take these tomorrow,' Wyn told her as she handed the pages over.

'Well, this looks very interesting,' Mrs Brompton said, 'my solicitor might be able to shed some light on these too. Thank you. Off you go now, it's almost dinner time.' As Wyn turned to leave, she said, oh yes, before I forget, as you have all been working extremely hard over the last few days, I think you should take the whole weekend off.'

'Oh thank you,' said Wyn, 'I'll tell the others, they'll be very happy.' Wyn skipped happily down the stairs back to the study. 'Mrs Brompton says we can all have the whole weekend off.' They all cheered loudly. 'We'll have to find somewhere to go she told them.' They finished off in the study and then went downstairs to prepare the dinner.

After dinner they sat around the table discussing where to go. 'Have you ever been to a big market?' Betty asked Wyn.

'No, I never have,' Wyn told her.

There was a livestock market with a few stalls selling vegetables and dairy products but that was all.

'Well that's one thing we can do,' Betty told her excitedly, 'I love Petticoat Lane Market, we could go there on Sunday.'

The others all agreed.

'How about Portobello Road on Saturday? There's always something interesting going on there, suggested William. There are some good Taverns round there as well.'

'Markets during the day and Taverns at night. That sounds like paradise,' said Betty and Ned.

The next day William let two Detectives into the basement. They had a close look at the skeleton, 'there was obviously a huge blow to the head,' one said, 'I don't think this was natural causes, I think we need the Coroner. He turned to William and asked him to make sure no-one came anywhere near the body. 'We'll arrange for the undertaker to come and pick it up and take it to the Coroner.'

'Do you know if it was male or female?' William asked them.

'Not at this point,' they told him. 'The Coroner should be able to tell. Does anyone in the house have any idea who it was?' they asked William.

'No, I don't think so,' William replied.

'Oh well, I suppose it might become clearer when we know what sex it was,' the Detective said. They started looking around the basement. 'Where exactly was it stored?' he asked. 'Rolled up in this rug in that room,' William told them. 'Show me,' he asked. William had taken the key with him as he thought that they might need to see inside. He unlocked the door and let them in. 'It was resting up against the back wall,' he said. They walked over to take a look. 'Can't see anything there,' they said, 'smells a bit musty in here though.' 'I think it must have been in here for quite a while,' one of them mused. 'Right we're finished, there's nothing in here.' They walked out of the

room. 'This is a very thick door' one of them said, 'it's like a prison door. I bet it's air tight.'
William showed them up the stairs and out of the house. 'Don't forget,' he was told, 'no one is to go down there until the undertaker has picked it up. It should be later today.'
'Alright,' William said, 'I'll make sure no-one goes down there although I don't think anyone would want to.'
When William went into the kitchen Wyn told him that Mrs Brompton was back and wanted to see them.
'She must of found out about George Brompton,' William said. When they got up to the drawing room, Mrs Brompton was waiting for them.
'Sit down she told them. As you know I have been to see my solicitor. He had a lot of information about George Brompton because he still corresponds with him. He is living in Jamaica on the sugar plantation and has been for a long time. He is the black sheep of the family and was a worse gambler than my husband.' He owed a lot of money to a lot of important people. It got so bad that he was called out in an illegal duel. When his father heard about it, he put George on the next boat to Jamaica before he could either be totally disgraced or killed. He is now living with an ex-slave black woman with whom he has two children and he will never be coming back to this country. Mr Brompton made financial arrangements for him in his Will which I will, of course, comply with. It means, she continued, that the body in the basement isn't that of George Brompton. I'm seeing the coroner later today so I might find out a bit more then. William, I would like you to come with me please.' Looking at Wynn and Betty she

said, 'you two can carry on with your normal duties until I know what is to be done next.' She asked William to be downstairs by two o'clock. 'Ned already knows and will have the car ready' she said.

Wyn and Betty went down to the kitchen and told Mrs Davis that they were back to their normal duties for a while.

'Thank goodness for that' she said. 'This house is not as clean as it should be so I want you to go through it room by room and thoroughly clean it. Wyn can start with the bedrooms while Betty starts in the sitting room. You've got two hours until lunch time so start right away.'

Wyn took what she needed out of the scullery and went up to Mrs Brompton's bedroom first. She changed the bedding and dusted and cleaned the room. She took the large rug from the floor down through the kitchen to the garden and threw it over the washing line. She started beating the dust out of it. William suddenly appeared, put his arms around her and started nuzzling her neck.

'Stop that,' she told him, 'I've got work to do.'

'Roll on Saturday,' he told her, 'who knows what we will be able to get up to then. He gave her a wink, pinched her bottom and then walked back into the kitchen whistling. Wyn just smiled to herself and carried on beating. When there was no more dust coming off the rug she took it back up to the bedroom. By the time she had finished she was very out of breath. 'I've had too much time away from this,' she thought to herself. 'I've got to get used to it again.' She went into the next bedroom which was Catherine Brompton's. This only needed a bit of dusting as it hadn't been used for a while. The next room was Charles

Brompton's and again, only needed dusting. She had just finished these rooms when she heard Betty calling her. When Wyn got back Betty told her lunch was ready and she was to take a tray up to the Sitting Room for Mrs Brompton. Wyn arranged a tray of food and took it up to Mrs Brompton who looked up from the letter she had been writing when Wyn put the tray down on a little table in front of her, 'thank you,' she said, 'could you post this letter for me?' she added. Wyn took the letter and went back downstairs,

'I'm just going to post this letter for Mrs Brompton,' she told Mrs Davis, 'I'll be back shortly.'

After lunch Wyn and Betty carried on cleaning while Ned and William went with Mrs Brompton to see the Coroner, Dr Jenkins. The entrance to the Coroners court was in the centre of the High Street and was in a building with the mortuaries and a post-mortem room. They saw Dr Jenkins in a small office next to the court. He told them what had been found during the post mortem.

'On inspection of the body, we found a smaller skeleton inside the larger one which means the person was female and pregnant. It looks like the cause of death was child birth as there is no sign of foul play,' he said. 'Why she had been left in a rug in that room we will probably never know,' he added.

'When did she die?' asked Mrs Brompton.

'It would have been at least twenty years ago,' he told them, 'although we can't be absolutely sure. The only way we will ever be able to find out who she was is if you can find some record of her in the house. The police are looking at all missing persons they have on record from that time but don't hold out a lot of hope. As she died of natural causes the Criminal Investigation Department are no longer involved so I'm afraid it's over to you. If you find anything out, please let me know,' he added. Mrs Brompton told him she would be happy to, thanked him and left. As they were walking back to the car she told William to tell Wyn and Betty to start reading through all the documents thoroughly.

'We need to find names of all the female staff around twenty years ago,' she told him. 'As it's Friday and I've given you the weekend off, tell them to start when they have finished their normal duties on Monday morning as Mrs Davis has been complaining that nothing is being done, the washing is piling up and the house is getting dirty.'

'We'll help them with the normal household cleaning,' William and Ned told her, 'so that we can get to the more interesting stuff a lot quicker,' they added. She smiled and said, 'I'll leave it with you then. Let me know what you find. I might remember some of them.'

CHAPTER FOURTEEN

They were all up and ready to go early the next morning. Wyn and Betty were wearing their best dresses and bonnets. Even William and Ned looked very smart in their best clothes. 'Where do you want to go first?' William asked them.

'I'd like to see Portobello Road,' Ned said, 'Mrs Davis mentioned it yesterday, she said it was a good place to go.'

'Alright,' the others agreed 'we'll start there.'

They went down to the station and caught a crowded train to Notting Hill. It was quite a long journey and took a long while to get there. They found Portobello Road to be a long, narrow street which stretched for over two miles. It was lined with a lot of shops, antique stalls, book stalls and even some food stalls.

'This is amazing,' Wyn said in wonder. 'I've never seen anything like this before.'

'Me neither,' agreed Ned.

They walked slowly down the stalls stopping to pick up items of interest. William bought them all hot nuts from one of the stalls which they munched as they walked. There was a lot of shouting especially from the venders selling fruit and vegetables. Wyn was fascinated by everything she was seeing and hearing. She grabbed Betty's hand and they went skipping happily along the road looking at all the stalls with William and Ned running behind them.

'Hold on you two,' William shouted, 'we can't keep up with you.' Wyn and Betty stopped skipping and stood waiting for them to catch up. They were out of breath and panting but couldn't stop laughing.

'I love it,' Wyn shouted, 'I don't ever want to leave.'
'I'm afraid you can't stay,' William laughingly told her, 'but we can come back often. Come on, let's find a tavern. I need a drink,' he added.

There was an old looking tavern on the next corner that they decided to try. They walked into a smoky, crowded, noisy room and squeezed themselves into a corner where there was a small table with, luckily, four chairs. William pushed through the crowds up to the bar and bought four tankards of ale. Trying to get back to the table with the ale wasn't easy and he had to shout to Ned to come and help him. They were both out of breath by the time they got back.

'I think we'll find somewhere else to buy something to eat,' William said. 'It's too crowded in here. Drink this then we'll leave.'

'If we can,' Betty put in, looking at another group of people crowding in. They started drinking their ale but kept being bumped by everyone around them. It was the last straw when Ned put his tankard to his mouth at the same time that a man was trying to push past and Ned ended up with most of his drink down him.

'That's it,' he exclaimed 'I've had enough. Let's find a less crowded place to get a drink in.' They managed to squeeze through the crowd and get out of the door.

'Phew!' exclaimed Wyn, 'I'm glad to be out of there.' 'Me too,' agreed Betty.

On the other side of the tavern was a stall selling meat pies. The smell of them was too much for Wyn.

'Do you want one of these?' she asked the others. As they looked really good and they were all starving they told her they'd love one. Wyn bought one for each of them and they found a bench and sat down.

'This is better,' Betty said 'at least we can move out here.'

'We haven't got a drink though,' moaned William.

'I can see another tavern down there, we'll try that one next,' Ned said.

Once they had all finished their pies William grabbed Wyn's hand and pulled her up off the bench.

'Come on,' he said, 'I'm thirsty, let's go see what this taverns like.' He opened the door and stuck his head in, 'it doesn't sound as busy, there's plenty of room in here,' he told them. 'I think everyone must be in the other one. This is much better. Come on girls,' he said, 'there's lots of tables free in here, we'll be able to relax.'

They walked in, found a table by the window and sat down. Wyn gave a huge sigh of relief. 'That's better,' she said. Ned got some drinks and they all just relaxed and chatted quietly.

After their third ale they decided that it wasn't worth going anywhere else as they were quite happy there and decided that this is where they would spend the rest of the day.

Wyn was looking around with interest as more people were coming in now but it still wasn't too crowded. She was so engrossed with the different people she was seeing, she didn't notice that William had been talking to her.

'Hello!' he said, 'are you still with me.'

'Sorry,' she replied, 'it's just so interesting in here. Look at that man and woman over there, they've been arguing for ages now.' Just as she said that the woman jumped up out of her chair, slapped the man hard around the face and ran out before he'd realised what had happened. He looked around sheepishly as everyone was laughing. He just shrugged and got up to get another ale.

'Why isn't he going after her?' Wyn wondered.

The others just laughed and Betty asked 'don't you know what that was about?'

'I thought she was his wife,' Wyn replied.

'No, not his wife,' Betty told her, 'I think they were arguing about her price.'

Wyn went very red in the face. 'Oh she exclaimed, I didn't realise there were women like that in here.'

'I can see at least four of them,' William told her.

Wyn started looking more carefully around her. She saw the four women William was talking about. Their faces were painted a bit more than usual but they weren't what she was expecting for a street woman as they were clean and well dressed. Betty saw her confused expression and told her that these were the more expensive ladies, that's why they were so hard to spot. It would be the more affluent men who went with them not men like the one she had just seen slapped.

After a couple more drinks they were all feeling a bit merry so decided that they had better start the journey home. They managed to get a train more or less straight away. It was less crowded this time and they all got a seat. William put his arm around Wyn and pulled her close.

'This feels nice,' he said as she snuggled closer to him. He put his hand under her chin and pulled her face up so he could give her a tender kiss. Wyn looked over at Betty and Ned who were both fast asleep. 'Look at those two,' she said, 'I think we must have worn them out.' 'They've had too much ale more like,' he replied. When they reached the station they had to shake the other two awake, luckily they only had a short walk back to the house. Ned didn't even try to talk Betty to going into his room this time as he was so sleepy, he just gave her a quick kiss and left. Betty walked into the house and straight up to her bedroom. William took Wyn into his arms and kissed her very passionately letting his fingers run over her nipples. 'See you tomorrow,' he said. Wyn gave him another quick kiss and walked up to her bedroom. She got undressed and got into bed naked. She could still feel William's lips on hers and his touch as he had rubbed his fingers quickly over her nipples. She let her fingers touch where he had, which made her body start to throb. She moved her other hand further down her body to the heart of her sex. She started moving her finger round and round while at the same time she took a nipple between her fingers and squeezed. A feeling of pleasure went through her body and she started moving her fingers around her sex faster. She could feel the sensations in her body intensifying until it felt like her body was exploding in pleasure. When she came back down to earth, she felt pure contentment and drifted into sleep with a smile on her face.

The next morning they all met in the kitchen. After Wyn and Betty had cleared away the breakfast things they all sat around the table drinking tea. 'Where shall we go today?' William asked them.

'I want to go down Brick Lane,' Betty told them. There's a lot of different things to see there.' I went once years ago and always meant to go back but never got around to it. She went on to describe all the places she knew down the lane, 'and when we've had enough of that,' she continued, 'there is a famous tavern in Wapping called The Prospect of Whitby.'

'I've heard of that,' William interrupted, 'sounds like a good idea to me.' He looked at Wyn and Ned. 'What do you two think?'

'Fine by me,' said Wyn.

'Yep and me,' Ned agreed.

'That's decided then,' said William, 'when we've finished our tea we'll go.'

A few minutes later they were all ready to go. 'Have a good day,' Mrs Davis told them as they walked out of the door. It was a lovely spring day and was quite warm with wispy white clouds in a bright blue sky. They all felt very happy to be out. They walked down to the station where they were lucky to get a train straight away. When they got off the train they had trouble getting through the crowds and out of the station.

'I didn't realise it was going to be so busy,' said Betty.

'Just keep walking,' Ned told her, 'it might be better when we get away from here.

When they finally managed to push their way through the crowds, they started walking down a long road with lots of stalls selling all kinds of interesting looking things. Wyn and Betty couldn't stop touching everything until Betty suddenly stopped walking and pulled Wyn into a shop selling bagels.

'I remember these,' she told them, 'you've got to try one'. She walked up to the counter and asked for four salt beef bagels then handed one to the others. Wyn took a bite, 'Ooh this is lovely,' she exclaimed, we've got to take some back home for later.'

At the top of the Lane were the stalls selling antiques, further down there were more stalls selling clothes, furniture, bric-a-brac, books and a lot more. The market was spread out along Brick Lane and spilled out onto the side streets. At the bottom there were some wonderful fabric stores. Wyn and Betty were still having a wonderful time looking at all the goods on sale but William and Ned were getting bored.

'We've been here for a couple of hours,' William moaned, 'let's go and find this Tavern you were talking about Betty.'

'It's a bit of a walk,' she warned them, 'but it's worth it once you get there,'

They started walking and ended up in the dockyards of Wapping. There were warehouses on both sides of the road and it was full of men with carts and wagons moving big bundles of goods.

'This is a bit rough,' Ned commented,

Just keep on walking,' replied Betty, 'it's just over there,'

'They looked in the direction she was pointing and saw the tavern. Wyn was relieved as she was getting tired.

They could see The Prospect of Whitby in front of them.

'Looks alright,' said William, 'let's go in and find out.'

They walked in and looked around them. The landlord who served them saw their interest.

'It's an old and historic tavern that was formerly known as the Devil's Tavern on account of its dubious reputation,' he told them. 'Unfortunately all that's left from the building's earliest period is the 400 year old stone floor. In former times it was a meeting place for sailors, smugglers, cut-throats and footpads.'

'What a wonderful story' said Wyn.

'That's not all,' continued the Landlord. 'In the 17th century, it became the tavern chosen by the hanging Judge Jeffreys as he lived nearby, there's a noose hanging by a window over there commemorating him. Even Charles Dickens and Samuel Pepys are known to have drunk here. There was a fire here that century and the tavern was rebuilt and renamed The Prospect of Whitby.'

Ned had stopped listening as he'd had enough of the history lesson

'I've started losing the will to live,' he whispered, 'I don't want a history lesson, I just want a drink, let's just sit down and have a drink.'

Wyn thanked the Landlord then they walked to the back of the tavern and sat down at a table overlooking the river.

Wyn and Betty looked out of the window at all the activity on the river. It was very busy with boats and barges taking people and goods up and down. There was a lot of shouting and Wyn even heard singing coming from the closest barge. She saw a woman doing her washing in a bucket on the deck. She was the one singing.

'This is amazing,' she said, 'they are living their whole life on a boat. I've never seen anything like it.'

They all jumped as the woman suddenly stopped singing and shouted at someone else on the boat. 'What are you doing? You stupid man'.

Wyn and Betty looked in the direction of the person she was shouting at. They were shocked to see a man, who was

obviously drunk, staggering onto the deck totally naked. He leered suggestively at her and started touching himself.
'Get your clothes back on you drunken old sod' she screamed at him. 'You'll be arrested if you're not careful,' She walked over to him and pushed him back inside. There was a loud thud as he landed on his back in the boat.
'I think it's just as well that we can't hear what he's saying now,' laughed Betty.
The woman had followed him down into the boat and a few minutes later the boat started to rock from side to side.
'Oh my!' exclaimed Betty with a knowing look on her face, I wonder what could be happening now.'
Wyn, William and Ned couldn't reply. They were all laughing too much.
'Well! exclaimed Betty when she had finally pulled herself together, 'I've never seen anything quite like that before.'
'Me neither agreed Ned. 'You don't get a lot of that in the country.'
'No, just murder, kidnapping and attempted rape.' laughed William giving Ned a shove.
Ned just smiled sheepishly but didn't reply.
They were all quite sad when it was time to leave as they didn't know when they would next have time off. They walked slowly back through the dockyards, fighting their way through the Dockers who had now finished work and were all on their way to the taverns around the docks. There were the sounds of women from the nearby flats shouting at each other and their grubby looking children who were playing in the street. William was holding on tight to Wyn's hand so he didn't lose her and Ned was doing the same with Betty. When they finally got through,

it was getting dark and they still had quite a way to go to get to the station.

'We'd better walk a bit faster,' William said, 'we need to get the train.'

When they finally got to the station it was completely dark and they were very out of breath. They had to wait awhile for a train and were all very relieved when they finally got home. Ned and Betty were whispering by the kitchen door and when William and Wyn were otherwise occupied, they slipped away to Ned's room over the garage. Wyn finally realised Betty was no longer by the door and said to William that she must have already gone in.

'Come on then,' William said, let's go in, it's getting a bit chilly out here.'

They walked into the kitchen but it was empty.

'She must have already gone to bed,' Wyn told him.

'Good,' he replied, 'we're alone at last.'

He pulled her towards him and put his lips on hers. She opened her mouth to let his tongue in and they started kissing with more passion. He slipped her shawl off her shoulders and moved his hand slowly over her body. She moaned as his hand moved up inside her skirt, up further into her knickers until it found her sex. He started moving his fingers round and round making her moan in pleasure. He took her hand and put it on to his very erect member. Do it he urged her, make me come, please do it, I need you. He moaned as Wyn took him into her hand and started moving it up and down faster and faster.

Ooh that's it he said, oh yes that's it.

As she moved her hand harder and faster he was moving his finger the same way. They both started to feel the pressure building until, as one, they bodies exploded in absolute pleasure. 'Oh Wyn, you make me feel so good, I really want you so much.'

'I know but we can't,' she replied.

'There must be a way,' he said. 'I'll have to try and find something.'

The next morning when she saw Betty she asked her why she had gone to bed without saying anything.

'I didn't go to bed,' Betty replied, 'I went back with Ned to his room.'

'Oh Betty,' Wyn said, 'what happened? You didn't did you?'

'Oh yes I did,' replied Betty 'and it was wonderful, better than I ever thought.'

Wyn looked shocked so Betty carried on.

'It's alright we were safe, you remember I had to go and take something for Mrs Brompton to Mrs Harvey next door, well, I got talking to one of the maids in there and she told me how to stop yourself ending up with a baby and that's why I didn't stop Ned, it was getting harder to stop anyway, we both wanted it so much so when we got carried away, I let him. I didn't mean to but couldn't help it. Oh it was so wonderful, I didn't realise just how nice it would feel.'

'Well tell me then,' said Wyn, 'how do you do it?'

'I'll tell you later,' Betty replied, 'all I will say for now is that it involves water and a sponge.'

That sounds a bit strange, Wyn thought, I'm not sure that sounds very safe. I think I'll wait to see what happens with Betty before I say anything to William.

'Come on Wyn,' Betty said, 'stop dreaming, we've got to get back to work and then look through the documents again.'

Wyn followed her out of the kitchen and asked, 'was it really that good?'

'Ooh yes,' replied Betty dreamily.

CHAPTER FIFTEEN

When they had finished their household tasks, Wyn and Betty went back to the study and started looking through the documents they had found to see if they could find any information about who the body in the basement could have been. They were looking at documents that were dated about twenty years ago as this was when the coroner said the body was probably from.

'There aren't so many,' Wyn said, 'we should be able to find her.'

'Here's one,' exclaimed Betty, 'her name was Mary Childs, she was only sixteen years old and disappeared twenty one years ago.'

'This is her,' said Wyn, 'there can't be any doubt, we'd better tell Mrs Brompton about her.' They went to the drawing room where Mrs Brompton was sitting doing her correspondence.

'Excuse us Mrs Brompton,' Betty said, 'we're sorry to disturb you, but we think we may have found out who the body in the basement was.'

'Come in,' they were told, 'tell me.'

'Her name was Mary Childs and she disappeared twenty one years ago,' Wyn told her.

Mrs Brompton repeated her name quietly to herself, thought for a few minutes and then said 'she must have been here before I was because I don't remember her. We need to find out more about her so I think maybe you should keep searching through the documents and also get William to do a further search of the basement. What was the document you found that mentioned her?' she asked.

'It was a copy of a letter from George Brompton to her family telling them that she was unwell so couldn't go home for the weekend,' Betty told her.

'I wonder what he had to do with it,' Mrs Brompton pondered, 'Oh lord!' she exclaimed as she had a sudden thought, 'I think it must have been his baby. It makes sense, that's why I didn't know anything about him. The family must have pretended he never existed, but did they know she was in the basement? Where was she before she died? They wouldn't have let her stay in the house. It means that there could be somewhere else down in that cellar where he kept her until she was in labour. Tell William I want to see him now please,' she asked Wyn.

Wyn ran down stairs to find William.

'Mrs Brompton wants you right now,' she told him.

'What for?' he asked.

'Just come on, you'll see,' Wyn told him.

They both ran back upstairs to the drawing room. 'You wanted me Mrs Brompton?' William said as he walked in.

'Oh yes William, I would like you to do another search of the basement, there must be another room down there somewhere. If you find one, I want to see it; I owe it to that poor girl's family to let them know what happened to their daughter. Start right now,' she added, 'take Wyn with you.' She turned to Betty and told her to go back to the study and find as many references to Mary Childs as she could. 'Go on then,' she said as they all were still standing there.

Wyn and William went downstairs to the basement. 'Alone at last,' William said, giving Wyn a quick kiss. 'Now, now none of that,' she said laughing, 'there's work to be done.'

William gave an exaggerated sigh and winked at her.
'Alright come on then,' he said. They walked down past the strong room where the body had been found and further into the basement.
'There's a door here,' Wyn told him. William opened the door but there was nothing in there.
'Not this one,' he said, 'keep going.' They walked through a long room with odd pieces of furniture in it. 'There's nothing else here,' William said.
'Hang on a minute,' Wyn told him, 'bring the light closer over here, there's another door hidden in the very back of the room. Look you have to turn the corner to find it.'
William walked over and opened the door. They walked into a large room that had rugs on the floor and wallpaper on the walls. There were tapestries and paintings all around the room. In the middle there was a large bed with a very fancy bedspread hung over the bottom of the bed. They went closer and noticed that the sheet on the bed was covered with large stains that could possibly be blood.
'I think we've found where she lived before she died,' Wyn exclaimed.
'I think you're right,' William agreed. 'Come on, let's go and get Mrs Brompton.'
They left everything exactly as it was and went back upstairs to tell Mrs Brompton what they had found.
'We've found a room they told her, it's definitely where she was.'
'Show me,' she said.
They led the way back down to the basement and took her to the room. She walked in and looked around.

'I can't believe he did all this and none of us noticed,' she murmured. 'How did he get it down here, he must have had someone helping him. What do you think?' she asked William.

'I agree with you,' he replied, 'he couldn't have done this alone.'

'Poor girl,' Mrs Brompton said, 'living down here all by herself and then dying alone. Alright I've seen enough,' she said, 'I'll let Dr Jenkins know tomorrow. He should be able to arrange an Inquest then. Come on shut the door and go and have your dinner.'

The next morning Mrs Brompton asked Ned to take her to Dr Jenkins office again and told Wyn, Betty and William to keep going through the documents once they had finished their household duties. They rushed through the cleaning and then went up to the study and carried on looking through all the papers.

'Put anything with Mary Childs name in one pile and everything else in another one. It will make it easier to go through,' William told them.

A couple of hours later they had finished. The pile with Mary Childs name mentioned was a large one. Wyn started looking through it.

'Oh my!' she exclaimed, 'there are letters here from her to her family telling them that she couldn't go home because she was now working as nanny to the children and couldn't leave them.'

'I don't think there were any children here at that time,' William said.

'Good excuse though wasn't it?' Wyn replied. 'There's other letters here from her telling them all about her fictitious life but never mentioning anything about having a baby.'

'Poor girl,' Betty said, 'she was probably only doing what she was told. Just think she was stuck in that basement for months not seeing anyone other than George Brompton, never going outside for any fresh air. I wonder why the letters were never sent.'

'I expect George didn't want her family to even know she was still here,' said Wyn, it's so sad. Oh my, she suddenly exclaimed.'

'What is it?' William asked.

'Mrs Brompton isn't going to like this,' Wyn told them, 'it looks like Charles Brompton helped his brother get the room in the basement ready for Mary and looked after her when his brother wasn't around. There's a letter here from Charles to George when he was on a visit to the plantation in Jamaica telling him how she was and that George should probably start thinking about coming back as it wasn't too long before the baby was due.'

'I've got another one,' Betty said,' it's a bit later and it's from George to Charles. George was back in London and Charles was at the country house. It's telling Charles that the baby had got stuck and Mary had died and asking him what he should do.'

'Are there any more?' William asked them.

'I can't see any,' Wyn told him 'but there's still a few more to look through.' A bit later Wyn said, 'here's one, it's from George to Charles telling him that he had taken care of the problem and that Charles was to put it completely out of his mind.'

About an hour later Mrs Brompton was back. William took what they had found up to her. She told him that Dr Jenkins would be back at the house the next day and William was to take him down to the basement and show him the room they had found.

'Oh, and while I remember,' she told him, 'I am expecting a visit from The Right Honourable Frederick Huxley-Chadwick some time so if he does come, please tell him I'll see him.' William showed her the letters they had found.

'I don't believe it,' she exclaimed, 'Charles knew about this all along but didn't tell me anything, that poor girl has been lying down there all this time and her family know nothing. I wouldn't of thought that Charles was capable of doing anything like this. When Dr Jenkins comes tomorrow, bring him to see me before he goes down to the basement,' she told William, 'there is no doubt that this is Mary and we have to let her family know so they can bury her properly. Go down to the kitchen now and tell Wyn and Betty that the Coroner will be here tomorrow. If he wants anything from them, they are to help him as much as they can,' she added.

William turned and walked down to the kitchen.

'What's happening?' Wyn asked.

William told them what Mrs Brompton had told him.

'I don't know how much we can help him,' Wyn said, 'we only know as much as you do.'

The next day the Coroner arrived and William took him up to see Mrs Brompton.

'Wait outside,' she told him. 'I won't be long and then you can take Dr Jenkins down to the room in the basement.'

She shut the door and William could hear a faint murmur

coming from the room as Mrs Brompton explained what she knew to Dr Jenkins. It was only a few minutes later when the door opened again and Mrs Brompton told William to take Dr Jenkins downstairs. Once they were in the basement room, Dr Jenkins gave William a large bag and told him to put all the bed clothes in it. William looked at the blood stained sheets and then looked at Dr Jenkins.
'It's alright,' Dr Jenkins told him, 'you won't catch anything.'
'Urgh,' William thought as he gingerly picked up the first sheet and quickly put it in the bag. After that it got easier to do and in no time all, the bedding was in the bag.
'Tie it up with this,' Dr Jenkins said handing him a piece of string. William tied the bag up and gave it to Dr Jenkins.
'If you thought that was bad,' said Dr Jenkins, 'it's about to get worse. I'm going to take this upstairs and put it in my motorcar. When I come back I want you to help me carry the mattress up.'
William looked at the very badly stained mattress and shuddered, but didn't say anything. While he was waiting for Dr Jenkins to come back down he looked around the room. Hmm, he thought, once everything is out of here it would make a very nice room for me to bring Wyn when we have some free time. I could make this look quite nice. When Dr Jenkins came back he threw a blanket over the mattress in case anyone saw it and took hold of one end while William held the other end. They carried it carefully up the stairs to the motorcar. William looked at the car doubtfully.
'Will it go in here?' he asked.

'I hope so,' was the reply. Dr Jenkins put his end in the front of the car while William was still holding it.

'Push it right down,' said Dr Jenkins.

William pushed the mattress right down into the well of the car. It stuck out a bit at the top but Dr Jenkins told him that it would do.

'Go and get the pillows,' he said, 'and then we are finished.'

William went back down to the basement, picked up the pillows and went back to the car.

'Right that's it,' said Dr Jenkins, 'I'll take these with me now but if I have any further questions I'll come back. Tell Mrs Brompton I'll let her know when she can contact the family so that they can bury her.

'Can I ask you a question?' William asked. Dr Jenkins looked at him and nodded.

'Can I clean the room up now?'

Dr Jenkins gave him a look as if to say I don't know why you'd want to but replied, 'yes it can be cleaned up now. I don't need anything else from there.'

William thanked him and Dr Jenkins then squeezed into his car and drove off.

William walked up the stairs, knocked on the drawing room door and went in to tell Mrs Brompton all that the Coroner had said.

'See if you can find Mary's family's address,' she told him. 'I want to be ready to write to them once Dr Jenkins says I can. That girl has been unburied for too long already. Ask Wyn and Betty if they found anything when they were looking through the study,' she added.

William went down to try and find Wyn. He found her cleaning the scullery on her own. 'Where are Mrs Davis and Betty?' he asked her.

'Mrs Davis isn't feeling well and is having a lie down and Betty is cleaning Mrs Brompton's bedroom,' she told him.

'Oh so we are alone,' he said seductively. He put his arms around her and kissed the back of her neck. Wyn laughed and shivered as a tingle ran down her back.

'Get away now,' she told him. 'I've got work to do.'

'Alright,' he said reluctantly, 'it'll keep. Mrs Brompton wants to know if you found any address for Mary's family when you were going through all the papers.'

'No,' she replied, 'but there are a few more letters to go through. I'll have a look this afternoon when I've finished cleaning.'

William pulled her close, gave her a long kiss then sighed and left.

Wyn finished her cleaning and then prepared lunch. While they were eating she asked Betty if she had finished her cleaning.

'Yes why?' asked Betty.

'There are still a few letters to look through in the study,' Wyn told her. 'Mrs Brompton wants the address for Mary's family so that she can let them know what happened to her. Do you want to help me look?'

'Oh yes,' Betty told her, 'I feel so sorry for that poor girl, I'd like to help her to rest in peace.'

Once they had cleared all the lunch dishes away and washed them up, they both went up to the study and started looking through the remaining papers. There were letters from a lot of people Charles Brompton owed money to and ones to people who owed him money. Wyn suddenly dropped a letter she was reading.

'What's wrong?' Betty asked her.

'It's from the new Manager of the plantation in Jamaica,' Wyn told her. 'I think it's my half-brother. He's thanking Mr Brompton for giving him the chance of starting a new life with his family in Jamaica because he never wants to go back to Penarth in Wales where he comes from. There's only one Henry Williams from Penarth. I wonder if he's told my parents where he is, not that I really care, he can go rot in hell as far as I'm concerned. At least I know where he is, he can't touch me from there.'

They went through a few more mundane letters until Wyn suddenly shouted, 'here it is, I've found an address for Mary's family.'

'Oh that's good,' exclaimed Betty, 'they'll finally know what happened to their daughter. It was so cruel of Mr Charles to go along with his brother and keep it all a secret. I wonder what would have happened if she'd given birth to a live baby,' she pondered.

'I dread to think,' replied Wyn, 'he couldn't have kept her and a baby hidden down there forever, someone would have noticed eventually. Let's take this to Mrs Brompton. She'll be relieved that she can put an end to this whole unhappy story.'

They went along to the drawing room where Mrs Brompton was having coffee and knocked on the door. Come in they were instructed. They went in and handed the letter over to Mrs Brompton.

'I think this is what you wanted,' Wyn told her.

Mrs Brompton looked at it and said 'yes it is. That's very good, once Dr Jenkins has finished I can arrange for Mary to be taken back to where she belongs for a proper burial. I would like all of you to attend with me. I know Hampshire is quite a long way from here but it can be arranged. Would you be willing?' she asked them.

'Oh yes,' they both replied, 'we'd like to say goodbye to her even though we never met her, it's so sad how she ended up'.

'Was there anything else of interest in the letters you were looking through?' Mrs Brompton added.

'There were just some from people who owed Mr Charles money and who he owed money to,' Wyn said.

Mrs Brompton just sighed and told Wyn to bring them to her later. Wyn nodded as she and Betty left the room.

'I feel quite sorry for her,' Betty said as they walked back down to the kitchen. 'Fancy having a husband like Mr Charles.'

Wyn shuddered and said,' no thanks, I'd rather not have one ever than have one like him.

'Or his brother,' Betty added.

CHAPTER SIXTEEN

It was a few days later that William answered the door to find The Right Honourable Frederick Huxley-Chadwick standing outside. William let him in and showed him into the downstairs reception room. 'Please take a seat,' he told him, 'I'll let Mrs Brompton know you're here.' He then went up to the study where Mrs Brompton was dealing with her correspondence.

'The gentleman you were expecting is sitting in the downstairs reception room,' he told her. Mrs Brompton slowly finished the letter she was writing before she turned at looked at William.

'Please take him up to the drawing room, offer him some refreshment and tell him I'll be with him shortly.' William nodded and went back down to the reception room.

'Please come this way,' he asked Frederick Huxley-Chadwick, 'Mrs Brompton will be with you shortly.' Once he had sat him in the drawing room he offered some refreshment.

'Get me a coffee,' he was told.

'Yes sir,' William replied strongly as he walked out of the room. 'What a rude man,' he remarked to Wyn when he entered the kitchen. 'He wants a cup of coffee, make it with dishwater or I'll spit in it,' he said.

'You can't do that,' Wyn exclaimed.

'Watch me,' was the reply.

Wyn made the coffee but looked away as she gave it to William so that she didn't see what he did with it. William took it up to the drawing room.

'I've got better things to do than sit here,' Mr Huxley-Chadwick said as soon as William walked in. 'Tell Mrs Brompton I do not like to be kept waiting.'
As William turned to leave the room Mrs Brompton walked in.
'It's alright William,' she said, 'you can leave now.'
William smiled at her sympathetically and walked back downstairs. 'Phew!' he exclaimed as he walked into the kitchen, 'I don't envy Mrs Brompton having to talk to him.'
'Don't you worry,' Wyn told him, 'I'm sure Mrs Brompton can hold her own against him. After all he owes her a lot of money.'
'Oh yes, I'd forgotten that. That'll take him down a few pegs.'
It was about an hour later that the bell rang from the drawing room. William went up and opened the door.
'Show Mr Huxley-Chadwick out and then come back up here,' Mrs Brompton asked him. William looked at him, he was a different man than the arrogant one who had entered the house. He now had a pasty pale face and was very subdued, Oh dear someone's had a shock he thought to himself. Serves him right. He took him downstairs and showed him out of the door. Good riddance William thought. William then went back upstairs to where Mrs Brompton was waiting for him.
'There's going to be a wedding,' Mrs Brompton told him. William looked at her shocked. Mrs Brompton laughed and said 'No, not me, I wouldn't marry that awful man. He has a son, Harry, who is much nicer than his father. Catherine has known him since they were babies and has always liked him. They are more like brother and sister but

I'm sure that will change. Anyway it's all agreed and Catherine is lucky that any decent man will marry her in the circumstances. Please ask Ned to have the motorcar outside the front door at ten o'clock tomorrow morning as I will be travelling to Surrey to let Catherine know the situation. Oh, and ask Mrs Davis to come and see me after lunch as there is to be a reception next week to announce the engagement and she will have to provide a buffet.'

William ran down the stairs, burst into the kitchen and said, 'you'll never guess what is happening now.'

'Judging by the way you just burst in here, we must be on fire at least,' Mrs Davis said.

She, Wyn, Betty and Ned were all sitting at the table drinking tea.

What on earth is it?' asked Mrs Davis.

William told them everything Mrs Brompton had told him.

'Oh my,' exclaimed Mrs Davis, 'that poor girl, fancy having no choice in who she marries.'

'Yes but she does know him well,' William said. 'Mrs Brompton said they've known each other since they were babies, it's better than having to marry a stranger I would have thought.' He turned to Ned, 'Mrs Brompton wants you to have the car outside the front door tomorrow morning at ten o'clock to take her to Surrey to see Miss Catherine, she will be away overnight so you will be staying there and, Mrs Davis, she wants to see you this afternoon after lunch as there is to be a reception next week to announce the engagement.'

At that moment the bell from the drawing room rang again. William stood up to answer it.

'She's obviously forgotten something,' he said as he walked out of the door. Entering the drawing room he found Mrs Brompton slumped on the floor. He ran over to the bell and rang it urgently several times. Down in the kitchen Wyn and Betty looked at each other,.'
I'll go,' Wyn said and she ran out of the kitchen and up the stairs.
'Bring smelling salts,' William told her as she ran in the door.
Wyn turned, ran back along the hall to Mrs Brompton's bedroom and grabbed the smelling salts from the bedside cabinet. Then she ran back to the drawing room where William had picked Mrs Brompton up off the floor and put her on the couch. Wyn waved the smelling salts under Mrs Brompton's nose. After a couple of minutes Mrs Brompton started coming round.
'What happened?' she asked groggily.
'You fainted,' William told her, 'how are you feeling now, should we call for the doctor?'
'No,' Mrs Brompton replied, 'no doctor, I'm alright now. I think it must have been the stress of dealing with someone like that nasty Frederick Huxley-Chadwick, he's not the easiest of people to deal with, but I soon took the smirk off his face.' She smiled at them and said 'it's alright I'm fine now, help me up.'
When William helped her stand up she said 'I'm actually very happy that Catherine will be settled. It's a shame he will be her father-in-law but I think he'll come off worst as she's not an easy person to deal with either.'
The next day Ned had the car outside the front door promptly at ten o'clock. As Mrs Brompton was walking

out of the front door she suddenly turned to William, who was showing her out.

'Oh no,' she exclaimed, 'I've forgotten to ask Wyn and Betty to get Catherine's room ready for her as she will be coming back with me. They also need to get one of the guest rooms ready as I think my sister, Constance, will be coming back with me and, as she never travels without at least one maid and a chauffeur, there will also need to be two servants rooms ready.'

'Don't worry Mrs Brompton,' William told her.

'Everything that needs doing will be done by the time you get back.'

Once the car had gone William went back into the house and told Wyn and Betty what Mrs Brompton had said.

'Well at least we've got a whole day to get the rooms ready,' said Wyn, 'come on Betty let's go up and see how much needs to be done.

When they had gone upstairs William thought to himself, hmm, now's my chance to have a good look at the basement room and see if I can do something to get it in a fit state for me and Wyn to use. He went down to the kitchen first to see where Mrs Davis was. As he walked into the kitchen he could smell the lovely smell of fresh baking. Mrs Davis was standing at the table kneading bread dough.

'Get away with you now she told him, I've not got time for chatting.' William smiled and left.

He looked all around to make sure no-one was looking, then opened the basement door and went down the stairs. He had already hidden all the equipment he needed to clean the room in a small cupboard under the stairs which he now retrieved. Since the Coroner had finished with the room William had kept the key in his pocket so it was easy for him to open the door. He went in and cleaned the room from top to bottom giving special attention to the bed frame because he knew Wyn was going to be a bit squeamish about lying on it after what had happened to Mary. Once he had finished cleaning he removed all the cleaning materials, locked the door and went up the back stairs to the attic room. He had seen some old mattresses up there when they were doing the house search. He looked at them carefully and selected the best looking one. Taking it back down the stairs he had to duck suddenly behind a door as he heard someone coming along the landing. The person was coming nearer and he thought, oh no, I'm going to be seen, how do I explain the mattress. Just as the footsteps got to the door he was hiding behind, he heard a voice shouting, 'Betty come quick, I need your help.' The footsteps stopped and started going back the other way and William breathed a huge sigh of relief. That was close he thought, it would have spoilt the surprise if Wyn had seen me but what I would have told Betty I don't know. William quickly took the mattress down to the basement managing to avoid any other shocks. He put the mattress on the bed and thought, well that looks alright, I don't think Wyn will complain about the room now. I just need to find some bedding and then it will be ready for our little love nest. Ooh I can't wait he thought putting his hand down and touching his now erect member. His need got more urgent and he undid his trousers and pulled his erect cock out. He was imagining what he and Wyn would be doing on the bed and his hand started moving up and down

getting faster until he came with a groan. When he had
recovered he adjusted himself with a smile and thought,
next time it will be for real with Wyn. He locked the room
and put the key back in his pocket. When he got back up to
the kitchen Wyn was just coming in with some dirty
bedding that she had taken off one of the beds upstairs.
'Where are you taking that?' William asked her. Wyn gave
him a strange look as he didn't normally ask her about
household things but answered, 'it's going into the wash
house so it can be washed, why are you asking?'
'I just wondered,' he told her while thinking to himself,
well that's no good, I don't want dirty bedding. He looked
around and saw they were alone so he pulled her towards
him and gave her a passionate kiss. Wyn kissed him back
and forgot all about his interest in bedding. When William
groaned and finally let her go, Wyn smiled at him and said
'I've got to get back to changing beds, I haven't got time
for messing about with you.'
'Can I help you with anything?' William asked.
'Well actually, I've got to move one of the beds so you can
help me with that if you like,' she replied.
'Come on then, show me what you want done,' William
told her. Wyn led the way upstairs to one of the servant's
rooms.
'In here she said, 'I need it moved from this room down to
the next floor.'
William got hold of one end of the bed while Wyn carried
the other. When the bed was in the room William asked,
'where's the bedding kept? I'll help you make the bed.'
Wyn went to the cupboard in the hall and took out all the
bedding they needed. Ahh, that's where it is William

thought, I'll wait for the right moment and take some downstairs. When they had finished in the room William turned to Wyn and asked, 'is there anything else I can help you with?'

'No,' replied Wyn, 'it's nearly lunch time so I've finished for now.' When Wyn had disappeared down the stairs William quickly nipped back to the cupboard and got out all the bedding he needed. He ran down to the basement room and put it on the bed. I'll make that later he thought.

CHAPTER SEVENTEEN

Now William had sorted out somewhere for himself and Wyn to be totally alone he was impatient to make use of it but circumstances seemed to be against him. Mrs Brompton had come back and brought Miss Catherine with her to get ready for the wedding. There was also Mrs Brompton's sister Constance Reade who had surprised them all by bringing her new husband to be with her. Mrs Brompton had only found out about him when she arrived in Surrey and it had given her quite a shock. It had also caused a bit of consternation when they first arrived as there wasn't a room ready for him, but Mrs Brompton had him put in Mr Charles's old room so it was soon sorted out. Wyn and Betty had been run off their feet looking after all of them. Constance was very demanding and was getting Wyn to do absolutely everything for her.

'I'm not a ladies maid,' she complained to Betty, 'I don't know how to do her hair or iron her clothes. She keeps slapping me when I get it wrong. You can do it better than me.'

'Go and tell Mrs Brompton,' Betty told her.

'I can't do that,' Wyn replied. 'Mrs Brompton has got enough on her plate without me moaning. I'll just have to do the best I can and Constance Reade will just have to put up with it.'

'You can practice on me for the wedding if you like,' Betty told her.

'Oh thank you,' Wyn replied, 'it'll really help me. Who are you getting ready?'

'I'm doing Mrs Brompton and Miss Catherine as Mrs Davis won't have time as she's having to prepare the food,' Betty replied.

'You'll be busy then,' Wyn said.

Betty just smiled saying 'Mrs Brompton is easy and she doesn't complain but Miss Catherine is difficult because she doesn't care what her hair looks like. She doesn't even wash it anymore unless she's told to. The life has totally gone out of her. It's like her life is over and she is just coasting along until it comes to an end. It's so sad. I'm going to try and make her have some interest in her wedding.'

'Poor girl,' Wyn said, 'but she's so young, she has to get over what happened to Frank Cooper. We're her age, it's up to us to try and get her to enjoy life again before her wedding.'

'Come with me now then,' Betty told her. 'I've got to go and see Miss Catherine now to talk about what her hair should look like. Let's try and get her to show some interest.'

Betty led the way upstairs to Miss Catherine's bedroom. She knocked on the door and they walked in to find Catherine lying on the bed just staring at the ceiling. She hadn't even bothered to get herself dressed and showed no interest when Betty and Wyn tried to talk to her. After a couple of minutes of trying to get her to acknowledge their presence in the room, Betty lost patience and suddenly shouted, 'Catherine look at me.' Miss Catherine jumped and finally turned her head and looked at Betty. 'We've come to talk about how you want your hair for the wedding,' Betty told her.

'I'm not getting married,' Catherine replied looking puzzled.

'Yes you are,' Betty replied.

'Since when and who to?' asked Catherine.

Betty looked at Wyn and shrugged. 'Your mother told you,' Betty said, 'you are getting married next week to Harry Huxley-Chadwick.'

Catherine looked shocked but not displeased. 'Oh yes,' she said, 'I remember now. I don't mind Harry, he's alright. Now Frank's dead I don't care who I marry.'

Now they finally seemed to have got Catherine acknowledging that she was actually getting married, Wyn left Betty to sort out how she was going to have her hair and went back down to the kitchen to carry on helping Mrs Davis prepare the dinner.

'How's Miss Catherine?' Mrs Davis asked her.

'She's getting better,' Wyn replied. 'Me and Betty are trying to get her used to her getting married and she seems to at least know now that she's marrying Harry.'

'Oh that's good,' said Mrs Davis. 'I feel so sorry for that poor girl.'

'She'll get over everything eventually,' Wyn told her, 'it's just going to take time but being married to Harry might help her.'

Betty walked into the kitchen and asked, 'what's for dinner? I'm starving, all this heart break makes me hungry.'

'Wait and see,' replied Mrs Davis slapping her hand as she pinched a carrot out of the pot. 'How's Miss Catherine doing?' Wyn asked Betty.

'She's not too bad,' Betty told her. 'She's showing a bit of interest now in how her hair is going to look and, she asked to see her mother. Mrs Brompton is in with her now.' Just as she was saying this, Mrs Brompton walked into the kitchen.

'Could you ask Ned to bring the car round to the front door at ten o'clock in the morning please,' she asked Mrs Davis. 'Catherine wants to go to the dressmaker to see about her wedding dress and also wants to visit Harry.' She looked at Wyn and Betty and said, 'I don't know what you two girls have said to her but she's a different person.'

'We didn't really say anything,' Wyn told her, 'she just seemed to suddenly accept that she was marrying Harry.'

'Well it doesn't matter how,' said Mrs Brompton, 'it's just good she's showing an interest.'

The next day was Wyn's seventeenth birthday but she hadn't told anyone so was surprised when she walked into the kitchen in the morning to start working, to find a cake with a candle in it sitting on the kitchen table. William, Betty, Ned and Mrs Davis were waiting for her and they all smiled when she gasped in surprise.

'How did you know?' Wyn asked.

'You told me when your birthday was a while ago,' Betty told her.

'I don't remember doing that,' Wyn replied.

'It was on one of our nights off when we had been out, I told you and you told me.'

Wyn thought for a moment, 'oh yes,' she replied, 'I remember now. I've written yours down so I don't forget.'

'That's what I did,' Betty told her, 'so that's how all of us know.'

'Blow your candle out and make a wish,' William told her. Wyn bent over the cake and blew the candle out thinking at the same time, I wish William and me could be together forever.

'Did you make your wish?' Betty asked her.

'Oh yes,' replied Wyn 'but I can't tell you because then it wouldn't come true.'

They all gave her a small gift. Betty's was a lovely scarf, Ned's was a handkerchief, Mrs Davis gave her a set of scented soap and William just said I'll give you a surprise later. He gave her a long look and walked out of the kitchen.

'Ooh!' exclaimed Betty, 'I wonder what surprise he's got for you.' Wyn blushed but didn't reply.

'Come on now,' Mrs Davis told them, 'it's time you all started working. Ned, you're supposed to be bringing the car round to the front door in about five minutes so I suggest you get going.'

'Oh no, I'm going to be late,' Ned exclaimed as he rushed out of the door.

Wyn went upstairs to start cleaning the bedrooms. There were more of them occupied now so it took more of her time to actually clean them all. She started in Mrs Brompton's room because she knew it wouldn't take long. Mrs Brompton always kept her room tidy. She knocked on the door and went in and was surprised to see Mrs Brompton still in there.

'Oh!' she exclaimed, 'I'm sorry, I thought you had already left the room.'

'It's alright,' said Mrs Brompton smiling at her. 'I'm just going, I was just trying to find this necklace for Catherine as her something old.' She opened her hand to show Wyn a very simple diamond necklace.

Oh that's lovely,' Wyn exclaimed.

'It's very old,' Mrs Brompton told her, 'it belonged to my great great grandmother and has always been handed down to the eldest daughter on her wedding day, I hope Catherine will wear it with pride.'

Later that day when they had done everything they had to do and Mrs Brompton, Catherine and the guests were at a dinner at the house of Catherine's husband to be, William took Wyn down to the room he had prepared in the basement. She walked in and looked around.

'This looks a bit different than the last time I saw it,' she said.

'I would hope so,' replied William. 'I've worked hard on it. What do you think?'

'It's lovely,' she told him.

William lifted her face up to meet his and kissed her gently. She put her arms around him and cuddled close. William kissed her again but this time she opened her mouth to let his tongue explore. The kiss got more and more passionate and William pulled her onto the bed. His hands started roaming over her body and she didn't try to stop him. He moaned and undid her blouse. He could feel her erect nipple underneath her chemise and pinched it between his fingers making her moan in pleasure. His hands then moved down to remove her skirt and undergarments until she was lying naked next to him. He looked down at her naked body and told her she was beautiful. Wyn just lay there totally exposed and revelled in his gaze. It made her feel very wanton but she wasn't at all embarrassed as this was the man she loved. William stood up and quickly stripped all his clothes off. She looked at his manly body with its large, erect member and a thrill went through her. William lay back down on the bed and ran his hands all over her body.

'Touch me,' he asked her and she moved her hands over his body feeling a shiver go through him as she did.

'Oh Wyn,' he whispered as she touched him, 'I love and want you so much.'

She reached up and pulled his face down to hers. She kissed him passionately and he sank back down on to the bed running his hands over her breasts and down towards her sex. His fingers touched her and her back arched as the pleasure shot through her body. Wyn was moaning as he removed his hand and started kissing her body starting with her nipples and then down until he reached the nub of her sex. The feeling in her body started building as his tongue moved in circles making her cry out with pure pleasure. She kissed his body, loving the salty taste of him, biting his nipples, then all the way down until she reached his erect manhood. She hesitated for a moment then took it into her mouth making him moan. She started moving her mouth up and down just like she did with her hand.

'Suck at the same time,' he groaned.

She sucked hard and he gasped.

'Stop, stop, I'll come and I don't want it to happen like that.

Wyn stopped and he pushed her down onto the bed. He started caressing her body again until she was moaning and writhing beside him. He got on top of her and entered her carefully not wanting to hurt her. She gasped as she felt him inside her, it surprised her that it hurt a bit, but once he was inside her properly and started moving it just felt wonderful. The feeling started building in her body again until she felt like she had exploded into a million pieces. She felt William suddenly tense and then he groaned out loud as he emptied his seed into her.

Afterwards they lay down together both completely content until Wyn suddenly jumped up, pulled on her clothes and told William that she would be back soon. She ran up the stairs and into the water closet in the scullery, grabbing a sponge on the way. She soaked the sponge with water and pushed up inside her as far as she could and washed everything out just like Betty had told her. When she had finished she went back down to the basement where William was still lying on the bed totally naked.

'Where did you go?' he asked her.

'I suddenly remembered what I had to do to avoid having a baby,' Wyn replied, 'Betty told me, but it has to be right afterwards or it might not work, but don't ask me what it is,' she added.

'Come and lie down again,' William said but just then they heard Mrs Davis calling Wyn.

'It's late, I thought she was already in bed,' Wyn said 'what on earth can she want at this time. I better go and see, you should probably get dressed too,' she told William.

William groaned but got up and started pulling his clothes on.

'You go first,' he told her.

Wyn gave him a quick kiss and went up the stairs. There was no-one near the top of the stairs and she managed to get into the kitchen without anyone seeing where she had come from. Mrs Davis was standing in the centre of the kitchen looking distressed.

'What's wrong?' Wyn asked her.

'I've just seen Betty sneaking out of Ned's room,' Mrs Davis replied, 'I don't know what to do.'

Wyn had to hide her smile. 'It's alright Mrs Davis,' Wyn said, 'I'm sure there will be an innocent explanation, Betty's not silly.'

'But they are so young,' Mrs Davis replied, 'they might be tempted to be do things they shouldn't'

'I'm sure nothing happened,' Wyn told her, 'they are both sensible people. Calm down and stop worrying, everything will be fine. Go to bed now, that's where I'm going.'

Wyn said good night and walked out of the kitchen thinking, oh dear I'd better warn Betty. When she got upstairs she knocked on Betty's door and walked in. Betty was sitting in front of the mirror thoughtfully brushing her hair. Wyn looked at her and laughingly said, 'you look like the cat that got the cream.'

'You don't look much different,' Betty replied. What have you been doing?'

'Same as you I expect,' replied Wyn.

Betty looked at her with a smile and said, 'really, you've done it and on your birthday too, where?'

'William cleaned up the room in the basement and put a new bed in there,' Wyn told her.

'Not the room where we found Mary,' Betty exclaimed.

'Yes,' replied Wyn 'but it looks completely different now, I didn't even think of it as the same room.'

'How was it with William?' Betty asked her.

'Wonderful,' replied Wyn, 'you were right, nothing we did comes close to the feeling I got with him. I didn't know it could feel so good.'

'Did you do what I told you to straight afterwards?' Betty asked.

'Yes, I used the sponge and water just as you said,' Wyn told her. 'I actually didn't come in here to tell you about what I got up to with William,' Wyn said. 'I came to warn you that Mrs Davis saw you leaving Ned's room and is now very worried about you.'

'Oh no, I don't want her worrying,' said Betty, 'I'm going to have to find a reason why I was in Ned's room at that time of night.'

'What time did he get back with Mrs Brompton and Catherine?' Wyn asked.

'Just before I met up with him,' Betty told her.

'Could Catherine have left something in the car that she absolutely needed to have before the morning?' Wyn asked.

'Well, I saw her before she went out and she had some diamond earrings on, maybe she lost one of them.'

'That's it exclaimed,' Wyn, 'she wouldn't want to leave that until the morning so she sent you over to see if it was in the car which of course it wasn't.'

'I'll tell Mrs Davis that first think in the morning before she even mentions it to me,' Betty told her. 'Thanks Wyn. I would have been stuck for an explanation if you hadn't warned me. I would never have managed to be alone with Ned again, although we are going to have to be more careful.'

The next morning Betty was already sitting in the kitchen when Wyn walked in. Betty looked up at her and winked. Mrs Davis was standing at the stove humming and looking a lot happier than the last time Wyn saw her. Mrs Davis turned round, saw Wyn and said, 'sit down, breakfast is just about ready, we're just waiting for William and Ned.'
Wyn poured herself a cup of tea and sat down next to Betty who just smiled and gave a slight nod. Oh good thought Wyn, Mrs Davis has accepted the explanation, that'll make life easier for all of us. Just then William and Ned walked into the kitchen together. They were both laughing and looked very happy and carefree. William walked behind Wyn, looked over to the stove to see if Mrs Davis was looking and kissed Wyn on the head. Ned did exactly the same thing at the same time to Betty. Wyn and Betty looked at each other and started laughing which did make Mrs Davis look round.
'What's so funny? she asked them.
'Nothing in particular' Betty told her,
'It's just a nice day and we're happy' added Wyn.
Mrs Davis just smiled and started handing them dishes to put on the table.
'After breakfast she told them 'you are to go up to the dining room and start polishing the silver. That'll take the smiles off your faces she added.' Wyn and Betty groaned but were still smiling.

CHAPTER EIGHTEEN

The day of the wedding finally arrived and the house was sparkling. Wyn and Betty had been working flat out for the past few days and were exhausted but proud of how the house looked. Mrs Brompton and Catherine weren't speaking to each other as they had been having huge rows that everyone in the house could hear. The atmosphere could be cut with a knife as Catherine wasn't happy with the wedding dress and was letting everyone know it but, as it was too late to change it, she was taking it out on her mother. Wyn was just taking some tea up to Mrs Brompton when the shouting started again. Oh dear she thought, this is not going to be a happy wedding. She heard Catherine saying 'it's your fault I'm having to get married, you could at least have got me the wedding dress I wanted.'

'There is only so much money,' Mrs Brompton replied, 'I know your father-in-law is paying for the actual wedding, but I had to pay for all the dresses so I'm sorry, but this is as much as I could afford. It's not exactly a cheap dress is it? It was made by the dressmaker who makes the royal family's clothes. How much better could it be?'

Catherine just gave her an evil look and flounced out of the door nearly knocking Wyn off her feet as she pushed past her. Wyn knocked on the door and walked in. Mrs Brompton was sitting on the sofa looking very sad.

'I expect you heard that,' she said.

Wyn nodded, 'she'll be alright once she's dressed. She'll look beautiful in her dress and when she gets to the church, she'll be the centre of attention so that will cheer her up.'

Mrs Brompton looked up at Wyn and smiled, 'you are right,' she said, 'Catherine does like all the attention on her. Go and get Betty, you can both help her get dressed.'

Wyn went down to the kitchen where Betty was sitting at the table podding peas.

'Mrs Brompton wants you and me to help Miss Catherine get dressed. We've got to try and take the sulky look off her face before she gets to the church.'

That's a bit of a job she's given us,' Betty exclaimed, 'she's being a proper little madam at the moment.'

'I know,' replied Wyn 'but we've got to try for Mrs Brompton's sake. Once the wedding is over Miss Catherine will be gone and we can all relax.'

Just then Mrs Davis came into the kitchen.

'What are you two whispering about?' she asked them.

'We're not whispering' Betty told her, 'Mrs Brompton wants us to go and help Miss Catherine dress and try and cheer her up before the wedding.'

'Good luck with that,' said Mrs Davis. 'Go on then, make her look beautiful.'

Wyn and Betty went up the stairs to Catherine's room. They could hear the sound of sobbing coming from inside, 'oh no,' groaned Wyn, 'here we go again, this is not going to be easy.'

Betty sighed, took a deep breath, knocked on the door and they both walked in. Catherine was lying across her bed sobbing her heart out. Wyn walked over to her and said, 'come on Miss Catherine, it's your wedding day and you don't want your face to be blotchy do you?'

'I don't care,' sobbed Catherine, 'I don't want to marry Harry, I don't want to marry anyone but Frank and he's dead.'

'Well, it doesn't matter who you are marrying then does it,' said Betty. 'At least you know Harry, you're not being married off to just anyone are you?' she added, 'not like Harry, he's being forced to marry you. He's really going to be happy with a sulky, miserable bride with a blotchy face isn't he?'

This shocked Catherine, she stopped sobbing and looked up at Betty. She hadn't considered that Harry didn't want to marry her. She looked in the mirror at her tear ravaged face. 'Can you help me look presentable?' she whispered.

'We can make you look the most beautiful bride in the world so that you will be admired by everyone,' Wyn answered. 'You just have to pretend it's the best day of your life to please your mother. This wedding is going to happen no matter what, but inside, you'll know you are just acting. You never know you might like being with Harry, he does seem very nice.'

'At least I won't have to live with my mother anymore,' Catherine said looking a bit happier. She sat and thought for a while. 'You know this might be a good thing, no mother to tell me what to do, my own household and, of course there's always the marital bed, that part of it could be very nice.' She was looking much happier now. 'Come on then, help me get ready.'

Wyn took the wedding dress out of the wardrobe. It was very fashionable, made of white silk with long sleeves and high neck. It had a train and a veil the same length. The veil was made of a very soft silk gauze and was edged with lace. It completely covered Catherine's face and wouldn't be lifted until after the church service. She had white kid gloves which went under the sleeves of the wedding dress and had a slit in one finger so that the ring could be put on the finger without removing the glove. On her feet she was wearing slippers of white satin with one inch heels.

'Oh you look beautiful,' Wyn told her when her hair had been done and she was completely dressed. Catherine looked at herself in the mirror with a satisfied smile on her face.

'I do don't I?' she agreed.

Wyn looked at Betty who had a worried look on her face and shrugged. Oh well, she thought I suppose this harder unfeeling Catherine is better than the sad weeping one we had a couple of hours ago.

'Well come on then,' Catherine snapped, 'let's go.'

Wyn and Betty took hold of the train of her dress and followed Catherine down the stairs where Mrs Brompton and an uncle of hers, who was giving Catherine away, were waiting. They both smiled at her admiringly but only received a glare in return.

The wedding party were going to the church in a carriage that Ned had hired for them. It was being pulled by grey horses and had very smart Liverymen. On seeing it, Catherine's mood improved even more and she even started smiling.

'That's better Wyn said to Betty, 'it might turn out alright after all.'

When they arrived at the church Harry and his best man were already there waiting for Catherine. As she started walking down the aisle Harry turned round to look at her.

His expression was one of wonder as he took in her beauty and he had a huge smile on his face. Sitting on the other side of the aisle, Wyn noticed his face when he saw Catherine and thought to herself, he looks like he has been struck by a thunderbolt, I think he's just fallen for her, poor man, she's going to rule him. Catherine, on the arm of her great uncle approached the altar taking her place next to Harry, her bridesmaids taking their places behind her. The clergyman asked her to raise her veil during the ceremony and she didn't argue, just did as he requested. Harry could now see her face properly and he looked enchanted with her. Once the ceremony was over, Catherine and Harry went into the vestry to sign the register, witnessed by one of Catherine's bridesmaids and the best man.

When they left the church Harry and Catherine returned to the house in Harry's carriage. The wedding breakfast was being held in Mrs Brompton's house. There were fragrant flowers everywhere and the house smelt wonderful. All the staff were assembled waiting to greet Catherine and Harry when they arrived back. Harry shook hands with all of them while Catherine just walked past them with a slight smile on her face.

'I'm not going to miss her,' remarked Mrs Davis.

There was tea and coffee waiting to be served from a side-table, and if required, it would be handed to the guests in teacups, leaving milk and sugar to be added to taste. On the table there were cold joints, poultry, game, lobster salads, ham, tongues, savoury patties, jellies, creams and fruit. In the centre of the table was the wedding cake which was large, elaborately decorated and thickly iced. When it was time to cut it, William handed Catherine a knife and she and Harry both put their hands on the handle and then placed it the centre of the cake. William then removed the cake from the table, and finished cutting the cake into pieces, then presented them on a separate plate accompanied by a small fork, to each guest.

When the cake had been offered to everyone, the toasts began. Harry's best man proposed the health of the Catherine and Harry extravagantly praising Catherine and her beauty which made her blush with pleasure. Harry then rose and thanked him for his kind words, complimented and raised a toast to the bridesmaids. Once the toasts were finished the ladies retired as Catherine had to change into her going away dress. She and Harry were leaving to tour Europe for three weeks.

CHAPTER NINETEEN

At long last all the wedding guests had gone and the wedding breakfast crockery had all been washed and put away, Wyn and Betty were just sitting exhausted in the kitchen with a pot of tea when the bell from Mrs Brompton's sitting room rang.

'Oh no!' exclaimed Wyn, 'what could she possibly want now?'

I'll go,' said Betty, 'it can't be anything much.'

Betty was only gone for a couple of minutes when she walked back into the kitchen. 'She wants to see all of us,' she told Wyn.

'Well William and Ned are both at the garage and Mrs Davis has gone to bed,' Wyn told her 'so it's just us two.'

They both went upstairs, knocked on the sitting room door and walked in. Mrs Brompton was sitting in a chair looking exhausted.

'Come in both of you,' she said, 'I just want to thank you for all your help in making today a lot better than it could have been.'

'That's alright,' Betty replied 'we're glad it all went off alright and Miss Catherine seems to be a lot happier.'

'Take the rest of today and tomorrow off,' Mrs Brompton told them, 'have a bit of a rest, I'm going out with my sister tomorrow so won't need you. Could you ask Ned to bring the car around the front of the house at nine o'clock in the morning to take me to The Ritz as I'm meeting my sister there.'

Wyn thanked her and then they both went back down to the kitchen. William and Ned were both in there sitting at the table having a cup of tea. Wyn told Ned what Mrs

Brompton had requested. 'I think after you've done that you'll have the rest of the day off like us.'

When they had all finished their tea, Ned asked Betty if she would like to go for a walk. 'Oh yes, I'd like that,' she told him winking at Wyn and they walked out of the back door.

'Bet I know where they're going,' William said smiling. He turned and looked at Wyn then grabbed her hand and pulled her towards the basement door taking a couple of candles with him. They ran down the stairs to their special room.

Once they were in the room William took Wyn into his arms and gently kissed her making her melt against him. She opened her mouth letting his tongue in to explore. She moaned as he pulled her closer to him, his hands caressing her back and then moving round to cup her breast. He pushed her slightly away from him so that he could pull the pins from her hair letting it cascade down her back.

'I love your hair,' he said as he ran his hands through it. Wyn let her own hands tease the curls on his head saying, 'I love your hair too, it's so soft and curly.' William pushed her down onto the bed, undoing her blouse and pulling it down over her arms. She gasped as his fingers took hold of a nipple and squeezed it hard.

'Take your skirt off,' he told her.

Wyn stood up and slipped her skirt down leaving her standing in her chemise and bloomers. She quickly took these off and stood in front of him unashamed of her totally naked body. William ran one finger down her body from her breast down to where her pubic hair started. She opened her legs slightly inviting him to touch her. His finger moved down lower and she moaned as he touched her. William pulled her down on the bed and then stood up to quickly take all his clothes off. He copied Wyn and stood naked in front of her. She looked at his erect member and put her finger out to touch him. She pulled the skin back and ran her finger over the eye pushing her nail into it making William moan. She then put her hands on his bum and pulled him towards her inserting her tongue where her finger had been. This made William jerk and moan louder. He lay down on the bed beside her and started putting small kisses all down her body taking special notice of her breasts and sucking on her nipples. Wyn could feel the pleasure building in her body but tried hard to stop it as she didn't want this to end quickly but when William reached the nub of her sex and started licking and sucking she couldn't stop it and her body exploded with such feeling she felt like she was floating. When she finally came back down to earth, she pushed William down so that she could do the same to him. She kissed him all down his body, taking his nipples in her mouth and sucking them. She reached his erect manhood, licked all down its length and around his balls, then all the way back up again. When she got back to the top of, she took him into her mouth and sucked hard making small enjoyment noises as she did so. William was groaning loudly with pleasure and tried to stop her as he knew he was close but she pushed his hand away. 'I want to do it,' she told him and carried on sucking hard, moving her head up and down along the length of him at the same time. She felt his body still and she knew he was about to come but carried on. She felt his body jerk and he cried out her name as his seed spilled into her mouth. Wyn swallowed and tried not to gag as the taste wasn't pleasant, yuk she thought, but she didn't mind because he had obviously really enjoyed it and she wanted to give him pleasure. They both lay back on the bed completely content.

'Oh Wyn, I really love you,' William told her, 'I want us to get married but I'm not sure how we can do it.'

'I love you too,' Wyn told him, 'I'd love to be your wife but servants can't marry each other can they?' she asked.

'I'll have to think of something,' William said, 'now I know you'll marry me.'

He turned his head and kissed her. Even though it hadn't been long his body was ready again and he ran his hands down her body. He touched her until she cried out for him to take her. He lay down on his back and told her to sit on him. She moved into place until his erect cock was underneath her special place and then lowered herself onto him. She could feel him inside her and she started moving up and down on top of him. William was writhing with pleasure underneath her and she moved faster round and round and up and down. She threw her head back in pleasure and knew she was going to explode. William started groaning louder and then stilled and jerked violently under her.

'Oh yes, oh yes,' he moaned 'that's good.' 'Stay there, don't move,' he said, 'I want to stay inside you for as long as I can.'

They lay like that for a long time, both of them dozing a bit. Wyn had forgotten that she was supposed to flush herself out straight away. When they finally stirred and made their way back upstairs, she suddenly remembered and dashed into the water closet hoping it wasn't too late.

When she came out Betty and Ned had joined William at the table.

'Make us a pot of tea,' Betty asked her, 'I'm parched.' She looked at Ned who smiled back at her.

'It's thirsty work,' Ned said and Betty blushed. Wyn smiled and made the tea.

The next day was warm and sunny and once Ned got back from dropping Mrs Brompton at the station, they all decided to go for a walk in the park. Wyn took William's arm as they walked. There were flowers all along both sides of the path and William surreptitiously picked a couple and handed them to Wyn.

'Oh thank you kind sir,' she said with a smile. Betty and Wyn had brought a blanket and a basket of food with them and Ned laid the blanket out on the ground and they all sat down. Wyn opened the basket and took out meat pies, some chicken and ham. They had also brought some bottles of lemonade to wash the food down with. The sun was shining and they lay back with sighs of pleasure.

'This is the life,' Wyn said.

'It certainly is,' replied William looking down at her. He leant down and kissed her gently on the mouth.

'Aah!' Betty exclaimed, 'that's sweet.'

'We're going to get married one day,' William told her, 'so you'll have to get used to seeing me do that to my future wife.'

'That's such good news,' Betty said, 'but how are you going to be able to arrange it?'

'I don't know yet,' William replied smiling, 'but somehow it's going to happen and we'll live happily ever after.'

'Well, I hope you do' Betty said.

William suddenly stood up and pulled Wyn up o join him.
'Come on you lazy lot,' he said, let's get a boat and go for a trip down the river.'
Ned and Betty groaned but got up.
'Ok,' Ned agreed, 'it could be fun but your rowing first.'
They walked down the river to where the boats were moored, William paid the money then helped Wyn and Betty into the boat.
'Well what about helping me then,' exclaimed Ned.
'You're big enough to help yourself', William replied.
Ned shrugged and jumped into the boat making it rock dangerously.
'Hey watch it.' Betty told him. 'You nearly had us over then.'
Ned just laughed and sat down next to her, planting a kiss on her nose. William took up the oars and started rowing them down the river. Wyn raised her face to the sun.
'This is the life.' she said. 'I could get used to this given the chance.'
William smiled at her and blew her a kiss. 'You never know what could happen,' he said. 'When we're married who knows where we could end up.'
When William got fed up with rowing, he handed the oars over to Ned.
'I think we should start back,' Ned told them. 'It's a bit colder now and I'm getting hungry.'
'Oh I see,' exclaimed William. 'It was alright while I was rowing but now it's your turn we need to go back.'
Ned just laughed. 'It's not exactly interesting is it?' he commented. 'Things are normally more exciting when

we're around.' He started rowing them back the way they had come.

When they had given the boat back they walked back to where the blanket and food was. When they had finished off the food, they all laid down for a snooze. It was a little while later that Wyn was suddenly woken up by screaming coming from the direction of the river. She woke William and the others up.

'Did you hear that?' she asked.

'Hear what?' asked Betty.

There was another scream.

'What could be going on there?' asked Wyn.

I don't know,' replied William, 'but I think we should go and have a look.'

They all ran down towards the river to where the screaming was getting louder and more urgent. 'What's going on?' Wyn asked a woman when they reached the river.

'A little girl has fallen in and no-one can get to her,' came the reply. 'Her mother can't swim but is still trying to go in and get her, the others with her are holding her back.'

William ran forward to see what he could do.

'Don't jump in,' Wyn shouted at him, 'you're not a strong swimmer.'

William didn't reply, just immediately jumped in to try and save the little girl. Wyn's heart was in her mouth as she watched him swim towards the last place the little girl had been seen. William dived under the water but came up with nothing. He did this three more times before he came to the surface holding the unconscious body of the little girl in his arms. He managed to swim towards the bank where Ned leant over and took the child off him. Ned handed her to Betty and then turned round to help William who was having trouble staying afloat. 'Grab my hand,' Ned shouted, 'come on William you can do it.' Wyn was standing watching willing William to grab Ned's hand. She could see he was very tired as he looked straight at her and mouthed, 'I love you.'

'William,' she screamed as he sank under the water. Ned jumped in and swam over to the last place he was seen and dived down to try and find him. After he'd done this a few times he had to give up and get out. Wyn was standing looking into the water with tears streaming down her face crying out William's name. 'Come back please come back,' she screamed.

It was getting dark by now and Betty and Ned took hold of her hands and pulled her away. They took her back to the house where Betty explained what had happened to Mrs Davis.

'You had better let the police know,' she told Ned.

'They'll have to make a search of the river to try and find William.'

Once Ned had gone she sat Wyn down and gave her a very strong sweet cup of tea for shock. She turned to Betty, Mrs Brompton's back so you'd better go and tell her what's happened.' 'She needs to know right away,' she said.

Betty walked slowly and sadly up the stairs to the sitting room and knocked on the door. 'Come in,' said Mrs Brompton. Betty went in and told her what had happened. 'Oh no,' she exclaimed, 'that's terrible. How's Wyn taking it? I know she was very fond of William.'

'She's in shock at the moment,' Betty said, 'they were going to get married one day.'

'Oh that poor girl,' said Mrs Brompton. 'Try and get her to bed and I'll come and see her later. Has anyone informed the police what happened?'
'Ned's there now,' Betty replied.
'How's the little girl William pulled out of the water?' asked Mrs Brompton.
'She's fine,' Betty replied as she turned to leave the room.
The next day there was a knock on the front door and Ned went to answer it. There were a couple of policemen standing outside.
'Come in Ned,' told them, 'I'll tell Mrs Brompton you're here.'
He sat them down in the reception room and went upstairs to the sitting room to tell Mrs Brompton.
'I'll come straight down,' she told him. 'Where's Wyn,' she asked as they descended the stairs.
'She's in her bedroom,' he told her.
'I'll go and see her when I've finished with the police.'
She walked into the reception room and the two policemen stood. 'Please sit down,' she said 'I presume you have some news for me.'
'We've found the body,' one of them told her. 'He had been swept a little way down river and was found by a couple walking their dog. It gave them a bit of a shock I can tell you.'
'Where is he now?' asked Mrs Brompton.
'He's with the coroner who will let you know when he can be buried,' the policeman replied.
'Thank you for coming to tell me,' Mrs Brompton told them, 'I won't keep you.' She left the room and told Ned to see them out. She then ran back up the stairs to her

bedroom and sat on the bed with tears running down her face. Is nothing good ever going to happen in this house she thought. How much more bad luck is there going to be. She knew she had to pull herself together and be strong to go and speak to Wyn. She stood up, straightened her back and took a deep breath then walked up the stairs to Wyn's bedroom. She took another deep breath before she walked in the door. Wyn was lying on her bed just staring at the ceiling. She turned and looked at her as she walked into the room.
'Have they found him?' she asked 'is he coming back to me?'
Mrs Brompton sat down on the bed next to her. 'Yes they have found him,' she told Wyn 'but I'm afraid he's not coming back to you.'
Wyn looked at her with pain in her eyes, 'he's dead isn't he?' she asked.
'I'm so sorry,' replied Mrs Brompton, 'he was swept down the river, he didn't have a chance.'
Wyn just nodded, laid back down and turned her head to the side. Mrs Brompton patted her hand and left the room.

CHAPTER TWENTY

It was a few days later when the coroner told them that William's body could be released. Mrs Brompton had decided that she would make all the arrangements for his funeral in gratitude for all the help he had always happily given her. She got Ned to drive her to the Funeral Directors and arranged for them to pick William up from the mortuary. She chose a pine coffin with a blue satin interior and brass handles. The funeral was to be held the following week. Mrs Brompton was letting the house be used for the funeral wake and anyone who wanted to attend would be welcomed.

'Do you know if William had any family?' Mrs Brompton asked Ned.

'I don't think he did,' Ned replied. 'He never talked about anyone but I think Wyn would know better than me. I'll get Betty to ask her, she seems to be the only one who can get through to her at the moment.'

When they got back to the house Ned went to find Betty who was in the kitchen making up a tray to try and tempt Wyn to eat.

'How is she?' he asked her.

'She's still not eating,' Betty told him 'but I'll keep trying.'

'Mrs Brompton wants you to ask her if William had any family who need to know what's happened.'

'I'll ask her,' Betty said, 'how did the funeral arrangements go?'

'The funeral is to be held next Wednesday Ned told her, 'Mrs Brompton has chosen a very nice coffin for him.'

'I'll tell Wyn nearer the time,' Betty told him, 'I don't think she's up to hearing about it yet but I'll ask her about his family.' Betty took the tray up to Wyn's bedroom and walked in the door to find Wyn sitting up in bed. 'Oh you look better,' said Betty.

'I've decided I can't just stay in bed and mope,' replied Wyn, 'all I'm doing is thinking about all the good times I had with William which makes me feel too sad. I need to be working so I'm going to get up and carry on as normal.'

'Mrs Brompton wants to know if William had any family,' Betty said, 'do you know of any?'

'He didn't have any,' replied Wyn, 'he told me he was an orphan with no family at all. That's why he thought me and him were so special,' she added with a sob.

Betty went to put an arm around her but Wyn pushed her away, straightened her shoulders and got out of bed. Betty decided Wyn was strong enough to be told about the funeral so said 'Mrs Brompton has arranged the funeral for next Wednesday. Ned says she has chosen a really nice coffin for him and the wake can be held here.'

'That's good,' Wyn replied, 'I'm glad he'll have a good send off, he would like that. I've got a lovely black dress I can wear so I can look nice for him.'

Over the next few days Wyn tried to carry out her normal duties but she really wasn't feeling very well. At least once a day she had to run to the water closet to be very ill. She just put it down to her not eating much and the grief she was feeling over losing William. She saw Betty looking at her very strangely a few times but didn't think much else about it. She was also very tired and had to sit down for a nap regularly during the day. I'll be alright when the funeral is over she told herself. It didn't even cross her mind it could be anything else.

It was finally the day of the funeral and it was pouring with rain. Wyn thought it was the right kind of weather for a day like today, the weather was as bad as she felt. She was dressed in her best black dress with a black hat, black gloves and black shoes. Betty and Mrs Brompton were dressed exactly the same. Wyn looked at them and thought, I'm not sure William would like all this black, he liked light and life but it's too late now. They were all standing outside the front door when the hearse with the coffin arrived. It was being pulled by two grey horses with black plumes on their head. Wyn cried out, 'William!' when she saw the coffin and rushed towards it. She laid her head down on the coffin where William's head would be with tears streaming down her face. Betty had meant to stay strong for her but this was too much for her and she couldn't help a sob escaping. She went over to Wyn and pulled her away.
'Come on,' she told her, 'it's time to go.' The hearse moved off slowly with an undertaker dressed in a long black coat and black top hat, walking in front of it. They all followed behind with Betty and Ned helping Wyn walk as she was so distressed. There was a short service before they were all standing around the grave for the burial where the vicar said a few words. Before the coffin was buried Wyn threw a single red rose onto the coffin and suddenly collapsed on the ground in a dead faint.
'Wyn!' Betty shouted and ran towards her. 'Help me get her up,' she said to Ned. 'Put her on the bench here.'
Ned put her down on the bench and Betty held the smelling salts that Mrs Brompton handed to her under her nose.

Wyn started coming round, 'Are you alright?' Betty anxiously asked her.

'I'm alright,' Wyn told her, 'I don't know what happened.'

'I've got a good idea,' Betty told her, 'but we'll talk about that later.'

She looked at Mrs Brompton who looked back at her knowingly.

Once the funeral was over they all went back to the house where Mrs Davis had prepared a light refreshment for them.

'I don't want anything,' Wyn said, 'I just want to go and lie down on my bed and be by myself for a bit.'

Betty helped her up the stairs and into her room.

'I'll be back to see you later,' she said.

Wyn just turned her head to the wall and closed her eyes. She felt overwhelmingly sad and tired and desperately wanted to feel William's arms around her but knew that would never happen again. Oh William she thought, why did it have to be you saving that little girl, I miss you so much and really need you here with me. She fell into a deep sleep and didn't wake up until a few hours later when Betty walked into the room with cup of tea and a plate of dry biscuits.

'Oh you're awake,' Betty exclaimed. 'Drink your tea and eat the biscuits before you get up. It'll make you feel better.'

Wyn did as she was told and had a sip of tea. 'I don't want any biscuits,' she said.

'I think you'll feel a lot better if you eat them,' Betty replied.

Wyn tried to get up but a wave of nausea came over her and she lay back down. 'What's wrong with me?' she asked.

'Do you really have no idea?' Betty asked giving her a knowing look.

Wyn looked at her and suddenly a thought came into her mind. 'No!' she exclaimed, 'I can't be,' she gave a broad smile as realisation dawned.

'I'm having William's baby aren't I?'

Betty nodded her head in agreement. Wyn put her hand on her stomach with a look of wonder on her face.

'William is going to have a son.'

'Or a daughter,' Betty put in.

'No, It'll be a son I know it,' Wyn told her.

'What are you going to do?' asked Betty.

'I don't know yet but I'll think of something,' Wyn told her.

'Maybe Mrs Brompton can help you,' said Betty. 'I think she already suspects so she might have some idea of what you can do. Now finish your tea and biscuits and come downstairs.'

When Wyn had finished and had gingerly got up they both went down the stairs to Mrs Brompton's sitting room, knocked on the door and went in. Mrs Brompton had been sitting quietly reading but put her book down when Wyn and Betty walked in the room.

'Sit down,' she told them pointing to a sofa in front of her. They both sat down and Wyn said, 'I know what's been wrong with me over the last couple of weeks and Betty thinks you've already guessed. I don't know what to do although I'm very happy that a part of William is going to live on.'

'I've been thinking about this all afternoon,' Mrs Brompton told her. 'I think I've got an idea for you. When Mr Brompton and I had the children we employed a nanny, Martha Reed, who looked after them for many years. She is a very nice and compassionate woman and I'm sure, if I ask her, she will take you in and look after you until the baby is born. You will, of course, have to think about what happens after you've had the baby but you've got plenty of time for that. Would you like me to go and see Martha and make arrangements for you?'

Wyn thought for a minute then gave her a big smile, 'Yes please' she replied, 'I'd like that.'

Mrs Brompton nodded and asked Betty to get Ned to bring the car around in the morning. Wyn and Betty left the room and went down to the kitchen where Mrs Davis and Ned were sitting at the table chatting. They looked up as Wyn and Betty walked into the room.

'How are you feeling now?' Mrs Davis asked Wyn.

'I'm alright,' she replied looking at Betty who gave a slight nod. 'I'm having William's baby.' Wyn told them.

Mrs Davis looked shocked. 'Oh my!' she exclaimed.

'It's alright,' Wyn told her, 'I'm not unhappy about it.'

Ned didn't say anything just kissed Wyn on the cheek and patted her shoulder.

'Mrs Brompton wants you to bring the car around in the morning as she's going to see their old nanny to try and arrange something for Wyn,' Betty told him.

'Oh that's good,' Mrs Davis said, 'at least you'll be taken care of.'

'Well you didn't think Mrs Brompton would just throw her on the street did you?' asked Betty.
'No of course not,' Mrs Davis replied, 'I'm just happy Wyn will be alright.' She turned to Wyn and said, 'we'll come and visit you a lot so you won't be alone.'
Wyn looked at them all with tears in her eyes and just said, 'thank you. I'll just have to think of what to do afterwards, although I've had an idea.'
'What's that?' asked Betty.
'I'll tell you when I've thought it through properly,' Wyn told her.
'One thing I've been dying to ask you,' said Betty with a smile, 'where did you and William go to be alone?'
'Really,' exclaimed Mrs Davis, 'that's very personal.'
'Don't say you aren't as curious as me,' Betty said, 'there aren't many places in this house where two people can be alone together as I know,' and she gave Ned a sidelong glance as she said this.
Wyn laughed and said, 'I'll show you one day.'
The following day when Mrs Brompton got back she rang the bell from the upstairs sitting room. When Wyn answered it Mrs Brompton asked her to sit down.
'I've spoken to Martha,' she told Wyn, 'she is very happy to have you staying with her until you've had the baby and sorted yourself out afterwards, in fact she says she is looking forward to having someone to look after. She has been a bit lonely since she retired.'
'It's very kind of her,' Wyn said. 'I've had an idea of what to do after the baby is born but I need to write a letter before I can tell anyone about it.'

'It's alright,' said Mrs Brompton, 'you have plenty of time before you need to worry about that. I've told Martha that you will be staying here for a few months yet, although I am going to employ another maid to help in the house as you can't do any of the heavy work anymore. Please go and tell Betty that there will be some girls coming to see me for the job of laundry maid tomorrow so she will have to answer the door. I'm also going to employ a butler now that my mourning period is coming to an end and I will be entertaining more, so there will be two men coming for that job too. Run along now,' she told her, 'I'd like you to bring me a cup of tea please.'

Wyn nodded and went down to the kitchen. While she was making the tea she told Betty what Mrs Brompton had said and that there would be girls coming for the laundry maid's job and two men for butler.

'I'm really going to miss you,' Betty told her, 'but I'll come and visit you often. It'll be nice to have new faces here though. After you've made Mrs Brompton's tea and taken it up to her we've got spare time so you can show me where you and William went.'

Wyn wasn't sure how she'd feel about going back to the basement room but told Betty she'd show her. Wyn finished making the tea and took it up to Mrs Brompton.

'Thank you,' she said, 'now rest for the remainder of the day, you've been through a lot recently.'

'Thank you,' Wyn replied as she left the room.

When Wyn got back down the stairs Betty was waiting for her. 'Come on then,' she said impatiently, 'show me where you went, maybe me and Ned could use it.'

Wyn wasn't sure how she felt about that but said, 'come on then, I'll show you.' She grabbed a couple of candles and led Betty down the basement stairs.

'Oh!' exclaimed Betty, 'it didn't even cross my mind that it would be down here, I thought it would have been up in the attics.'

Wyn led her to the hidden room and lit the extra candles they had left in there. She heard Betty give a sharp intake of breath as she took in the look of the room.

'Oh my,' she said, 'you've made this room look very cosy and nice.'

Wyn was just standing in the doorway looking at the bed, memories of how it had been with William were running through her mind, she could see Betty's mouth moving but wasn't listening to a word she was saying. She walked over to the bed and picked up the pillow where William's head had been and put it to her face. She could smell him on it and held it tightly to her body. Betty stopped talking and watched her with concern. Wyn sat down on the bed still cuddling the pillow and ran her hand down the length of the bed, she lay down sobbing and calling William's name.

'Oh I'm so sorry I got you to do this,' Betty told her, 'I didn't think how it would upset you. Come on let's leave now and get you upstairs, it must be time for dinner now.'

Wyn didn't move just kept sobbing.

'Come on Wyn,' Betty said, 'it'll make you ill if you keep on like this, think of the baby, you'll upset him.'

The sobbing stopped abruptly at this and Wyn sat up.

'Yes,' she said, 'you're right, I've got to think of William's baby now, not just of myself.'

Betty blew out the candles and led Wyn out of the room. 'I don't think Ned and me will be using this room after all,' she told Wyn, 'it means too much to you.'

'No, please use it,' Wyn replied, 'it's a happy room, I'd like to think it's still being used as a love nest. Make it yours and Ned's room.'

'Alright,' Betty told her, 'I'll take Ned down there and see what he thinks, if he likes it, we'll make it our own.'

'Good, that's that settled then,' Wyn said, 'because I'll never come down here again.' She took one more look around and walked up the stairs.

After dinner Wyn went up to her room and sat down at a table that was in front of the window. She looked out at the street below and thought about how her life was about to change again. She picked up her pen and started to write the most important letter of her life. I hope this works she thought, I don't know what I'm going to do if it doesn't. When she had finished writing she took it downstairs and put it on the hall table. Ned picked up the post there every morning and took it to the post office. As she was walking back up the stairs, she saw Ned kissing Betty goodnight outside the kitchen door. Betty had just shown him the basement room.

'What did he think?' Wyn asked her when Ned had left.

'He liked it,' replied Betty. 'We're going to get our own bed linen for the bed and put a couple of pictures Ned has on the walls so it will be our room.'

'That's good,' Wyn told her, 'I'm glad it's still going to be used but be more careful than I was, you don't want to end up like me.'

'I know I'll be careful,' Betty replied. 'Come and sit down for a while with me,' Betty said, 'I won't be able to talk to you every day for much longer.'
'No, but you'll have Ned and the new maid,' Wyn replied.
'I know,' said Betty, 'but it won't be the same without you. We've been through a lot of things together, especially at the house in the country.'
'Oh yes, I'd forgotten about that,' Wyn said, 'a lot went on then with murder and suicide'
'And don't forget Miss Catherine being kidnapped,' put in Betty.
They both laughed as Betty reminded Wyn about seeing Mr Charles naked in the barn with the farmer's wife.
'What a sight that was,' said Wyn still laughing. Just then Mrs Davis came in.
'Come on you two,' she said, 'time you were both in bed.'
They both said goodnight and walked up the stairs still laughing. 'Goodnight,' Betty said as they reached her room. 'Goodnight,' replied Wyn kissing her on the mouth.
'I won't be doing that with anyone else,' Betty told her.
'Me neither,' agreed Wyn.

CHAPTER TWENTY ONE

The next day was very busy with people coming to the house for the vacant positions. Mrs Brompton employed a young laundry maid called Molly and a new Butler whose name was Patrick Broome. Molly was sixteen years old and came from the east end of London. She had a mop of red hair with freckles all over her face and seemed very jolly. Mr Broome was very tall and slim with dark hair and didn't have any kind of accent when he talked. Betty told Wyn all this when they met up in the kitchen.

'Did you see Mrs Brompton today?' she asked her, 'she's out of mourning dress and is dressed in much brighter clothes. The gloom that has hung over this house for months is finally lifting and with any luck things are going to get much happier around here.'

'I hope so for your sake,' Wyn told her.

'Oh I've just remembered Mrs Brompton wants to see us after lunch' Betty told her.

They could hear laughter coming from the kitchen as they went down the stairs for lunch. As they walked in Mrs Davis was laughing at something Molly had just told her. Wyn and Betty looked at each other in surprise. Mrs Davis wasn't known for her sense of humour.

After lunch they were all called up to the sitting room where Mrs Brompton was waiting for them.

'I just wanted to tell you what the new situation is regarding your duties,' she told them. 'As you know we now have Molly and Patrick Broome working here. Molly will be working in the laundry room doing all the household washing and ironing, Betty, you will now be doing all the cleaning around the house which leaves Wyn, as you are having a baby, your duties will be a lot lighter. You will spend all the remaining time you have before you leave us, in the kitchen helping Mrs Davis with the cooking.' She looked at Mrs Davis, 'I take it this is alright with you.'

'Of course it is,' Mrs Davis replied, 'I'll be glad of the help.'

'I think you'll need help,' Mrs Brompton told her with a smile, 'as I'm no longer in mourning I intend to have a lot of house parties and receptions. This house is going to be happy again. There is one more thing, as we still don't have a lot of maids in the house, each of you will be responsible for cleaning your own rooms except of course for Mr Broome. As he is the butler I would like Betty to clean his room for him. Have any of you got any questions?' None of them did so she said, 'alright go and carry on as normal.'

The days and weeks passed quickly, Wyn was getting larger and was finding it harder to do anything. She also needed to rest a lot and knew it wouldn't be long before she would have to leave the house which made her feel very sad. She'd had a reply to her letter but hadn't told anyone yet what had been arranged for after the baby was born. Then the day she had been dreading arrived and Mrs Brompton called her up to her room.

'You know you can't carry on much longer,' Mrs Brompton told her. 'I know it's getting harder for you so I've arranged with Martha that you will move in with her in two weeks time.'

Wyn's head dropped sadly but she agreed that she would be ready to go then.

'Ned will take you and your belongings in the car and we will have a small get together before you leave.'

'Thank you for everything,' Wyn said, 'I don't know what I would have done if it wasn't for you, I'll never work for anyone as nice as you.'

Mrs Brompton looked embarrassed at this and told Wyn to go now and rest.

The day before Wyn was due to leave, Mrs Brompton gathered them all together to say goodbye to Wyn. Mrs Davis had prepared a few snacks for them and Mrs Brompton provided them with a glass of sherry.

'You know we are here to say goodbye and good luck to Wyn,' she said giving her a parcel. 'This is from me she told her, it's just something I kept from when Catherine was a baby, it might come in handy for you.'

Wyn opened it to find a whole pile of baby clothes.

'Oh thank you,' she said 'this is so good of you. I hadn't even thought about baby clothes yet.'

Betty also gave her a gift of clothes.

'These are from Mrs Davis, Ned and me,' she told her.

Wyn had tears streaming down her face now and could no longer speak.

'Thank you,' she whispered, 'you're all so kind.'

'It's about time you told us what your plans are,' Betty said, 'I want to know you're going to be alright.'

'It's all arranged,' Wyn told them, 'once the baby is born and old enough to travel, my sister and her husband are going to come and take him back to Wales to live with them. They have been trying to have a baby of their own for a long time but nothing is happening, so I asked them if they wanted to adopt my baby and they really do.'

Her voice broke a bit but she carried on, 'I don't want mine and William's baby to have a poor life and I know I wouldn't be able to give him much. At least this way I'll know he is well looked after and will be able to see him sometimes.'

'Will he know you're his mother?' asked Betty.

'No, he'll think I'm just his aunt,' replied Wyn. 'It's for the best.'

By now Wyn was really sobbing so Mrs Brompton whispered to Betty that she should take Wyn to her bedroom and let her have a lie down quietly by herself. Once she was in her room Betty gave her a long hug until she had stopped crying, then kissed her on the lips and left her to sleep.

The next day Wyn was standing in the hall with all her belongings waiting for Ned to come with the car. Betty, Mrs Davis and Mrs Brompton were all standing with her.

'I'll say goodbye now,' Mrs Brompton told her, 'I'll leave Betty to see you off.' She kissed her on the cheek, 'take care of yourself and your baby,' she said, 'I've told Martha to let me know how you get on.'

Mrs Davis kissed her as well and said, 'I'll leave you too, good luck with everything, I hope you find happiness in your life.'

Then there was just Wyn and Betty. They hugged and Betty said, 'I'll come and see you soon. Ned will know where you are.'

Just then Ned came in the door and told them the car was outside.

'Come on,' he said, 'don't hang around, it'll only make it harder to leave.'

Betty kissed her again and ran up the stairs crying. Wyn looked around for one last time.

'Alright I'm ready now,' she told Ned.

Ned put all her belongings in the car and helped Wyn in. As the car moved off, Wyn didn't look back but stared straight ahead dry eyed.

CHAPTER TWENTY TWO

Wyn didn't take any notice of where they were going as she spent the whole journey in tears. When she felt the car stop she wiped her eyes, sat up and looked around her.
'Where are we?' she asked Ned.
'North London,' he replied, 'to be exact, Willesden.'
'How far away from the house is that?' she asked.
'Far enough,' he told her.
'How's Betty going to visit me if it's that far?' she asked him tearfully.
'It's alright,' Ned soothed, patting her hand, 'I'll bring her now I know where it is.'
Wyn turned and looked at the front door as she heard it open. A very plump, jolly looking woman was standing on the front step with a wide smile on her face. She came down to greet them.
'You must be Wyn,' she said giving her a huge hug, 'I'm very glad to see you. I've been looking forward to you arriving, I get quite lonely by myself. It'll be nice to have company for a while until you get yourself sorted. Come on in, you must be exhausted. I'll show you your room,' she turned to Ned and told him to follow them with Wyn's belongings.
She lived in a small neat and tidy looking terraced house with a well scrubbed door step. Wyn walked in to a very bright and clean hall. There were stairs to the right of the door that Martha now led Wyn and Ned up and flowered wall paper on the wall up the stairs and along the landing. At the top of the stairs Martha walked past the first door and opened the second.

'This is your room,' she told Wyn. 'The bathroom is the door down the end of the landing. That's all you need to know for now. Put your things away, there's plenty of cupboards to put things in, then when you've finished come down, I'll make you a cup of tea. Wyn thanked her then looked around the room.

'It's nice isn't it? Ned asked her.

Wyn jumped as she'd forgotten he was still there.

'Yes it is,' she replied.

'I know it's all very strange but you will get used to being here,' Ned said, 'she does seem very nice.'

'Yes I know,' Wyn replied, 'but I'm going to miss all of you.'

Ned pulled her towards him and hugged her.

'We'll miss you too,' he said, 'but we will come and see you.'

Just then the baby decided to give a hefty kick, Ned jumped back and looked down at Wyn's stomach in awe. 'Oh' he exclaimed, 'he kicked me.'

'He must like the sound of your voice,' Wyn told him smiling.

Ned put his hand on her stomach then kissed her on the cheek and said 'I've got to go now, Mrs Brompton might need me.'

Wyn's head sank to her chest, 'I know' she said in a small voice, 'I'll be alright, tell Betty I miss her already.'

She gave a slight smile as Ned turned round and left. She sank down onto the bed and put her head in her hands. Martha found her sitting like that when she came looking for her ten minutes later.

'Come on lovey,' she said putting her arm around her, 'come and have some tea. It'll be alright. Things will get better.'

Wyn let herself be led out of the room and down the stairs into a very large kitchen. She looked around her with interest.

'Not bad is it,' Martha asked her. 'It was the thing I liked best about this house when Mrs Brompton found it for me.' Wyn sat down and found herself showing more interest in where she was and who she was going to be living with for the next few months.

Over the next few days, Wyn got to know Martha and found her to be a very happy and friendly woman who would do anything to make her life easier. She knew she was going to be well looked after until the baby was born, although Wyn found life dragging a bit because she didn't have a lot to occupy herself with. She hadn't had any visitors yet and was really missing Betty and Ned. She even found herself missing being shouted at by Mrs Davis and all the work she used to have to do. Martha was trying her best to keep her mind off the loss of William and her friends by spending a lot of time with her but it wasn't the same. After a couple of weeks of trying to keep her spirits up, Martha brought her cousin, Tommy Cliffe, back to the house with her as she thought that maybe he could keep Wyn company for a while. She had told him all about Wyn and what had happened to William. He was a little older than Wyn but she found that didn't matter as he was such a nice person, and so handsome, she thought to herself. He owned a confectioners shop just around the corner and made her laugh with the stories he told her about the people that came in and the strange things they did. He made the days more interesting for her and she even found herself laughing, which was something she hadn't done for a long time. He started coming round to the house more often and Wyn knew that he liked her a lot. He didn't seem to mind that she was expecting a baby and wasn't married. I really like him too she thought to herself.

The next few weeks passed happily although Wyn could no longer see her feet and had trouble walking as she had got so big. The baby was due any time now and Wyn couldn't wait for it to be over as she was very uncomfortable. She was sitting in the parlour one day doing some sewing when she heard the front door bell ring. A few minutes later the parlour door opened and Wyn looked up to see Betty standing in front of her.

'Betty,' she cried, 'oh I'm so glad to see you, I've missed you so much.'

Betty put her arms around her to give her a hug.

'Look at you!' she exclaimed laughing, 'you've really got big, I can't even get my arms around you, but I've really missed you too.' She gave her a big kiss.

'Sit down, tell me what's been happening since I've been gone,' Wyn asked. 'I've missed everyone so much'.

'Well, you won't believe it, but Mrs Brompton is getting married again. She's met a very nice man who loves her very much. We all like him and he's not going to change anything in the house, so we're all happy. She's become a grandmother as Miss Catherine had a daughter who is very sweet. She's very happy too. Me and Ned are going to get married one day as well. Mrs Brompton has told us we can live in the flat above the garage and I want you to be my attendant.'

Wyn clapped her hands in excitement, 'ooh yes I'd like that,' Wyn told her, 'just tell me when and I'll be there. I might even have someone to bring with me.'

Betty looked at her in shock, 'who?' she asked. 'How could you have met someone being stuck in here?'

'He's Martha's nephew,' Wyn told her, 'and he's very nice, you'll like him. He owns a confectioners shop and I'll be going to work there for him when this baby finally comes out. Martha has said that I can carry on living here with her. How long will you be able to stay?'

'I'm spending the night here,' Martha arranged it all.

'She's putting a mattress in your room so we can spend time together,' Betty told her.

There was a knock on the door and Martha walked in with a tray holding a teapot, a couple of cups and saucers and some biscuits. Wyn struggled out of the chair, waddled over to her and gave her a hug.

'You are so kind she told her,' with tears in her eyes. 'Thank you so much for arranging this.'

Martha blushed in pleasure, 'you're very welcome,' she said.

They spent the rest of the day talking over old times and just enjoying being together again. Betty told Wyn all about the arrangements for her wedding to Ned. They were getting married in the church around the corner from the house and Mrs Davis was doing the food for the wedding breakfast that Mrs Brompton was letting them have. They would then set up home in the flat above the garage and Ned would carry on being the chauffeur although Betty would no longer work in the house. Wyn suddenly gasped and held her stomach.

'What is it?' Betty asked,' is it the baby?'

Wyn nodded staying very calm, 'go and get Martha,' she said, 'I think this baby wants to see you too.'

Betty ran down the hall shouting for Martha.

'What is it?' Martha asked.

'The baby's coming,' Betty told her, 'what should I do?'

'Go back to Wyn,' Martha told her, 'I'll run and get the midwife.'

Betty went back to Wyn who was now lying on the floor moaning in pain. She felt a sudden wetness running down her legs. She started to panic a bit, 'my waters have gone,' she exclaimed, 'I hope the midwife comes soon, I think this is going to be too quick.'

Betty sat down next to her, 'keep calm and hold my hand she told her, it'll be alright, I'm with you.'

Wyn grabbed hold of Betty's hand and squeezed very hard as she felt the next contraction. She was holding onto Betty's hand so tightly that Betty had to bite her lip so she wouldn't cry out with pain.

'I wish William was here,' Wyn cried out when the pain had passed.

Betty nodded, 'I know but you just have to make do with me.'

Wyn smiled through the pain, 'I'm so glad you're here.' She gasped as she felt another contraction.

'They're happening a bit closer together,' Betty told her, 'I don't think it's going to be much longer. Where's that midwife.'

'Betty quick, it's too late for that,' Wyn shouted, 'I can feel the baby coming. Help me take my underclothes off.'
Betty helped her out of her knickers and looked down,
'I can see the head,' she cried, 'push slowly so I can help it slide out.'
Wyn pushed slowly.
'Stop for a minute,' Betty told her, 'I need to turn it, that's it now push hard.'
Wyn pushed and the baby slid out.
'It's a boy,' cried Betty, 'oh he's lovely Wyn, well done, you did it.'
The midwife rushed through the door and took in the scene.
'That was quick,' she exclaimed, 'let's have a look at you.' She cut the cord, picked the baby us and wrapped him in a blanket.
'He looks fine,' she said handing him to Betty. 'Hold him for a minute while I finish things off with Wyn.' She inspected the afterbirth to make sure nothing had been left behind and then told them that everything was fine. She then took the baby back off Betty, weighed him and had a good look at him. She put him in Wyn's arms.
'Put him against your breast,' she told Wyn.
Wyn put his mouth against her nipple and gasped as he took it into his mouth and started sucking. The midwife looked up at Betty, 'you did a good job, 'she told her.
'I'm just so glad you were here,' Wyn told Betty, 'thank you.'
'I wouldn't have missed it,' Betty told her. 'I've never seen a baby born before, it was amazing.'
'I hope it hasn't put you off,' the midwife said.
'It didn't look too bad to me,' Betty answered.

The midwife just looked at her, smiled but said nothing. After the midwife had gone and the baby had been fed, dressed and settled in his moses basket Betty turned to Wyn and asked her if she was sure she still wanted to give him to her sister.

'I'm sure,' Wyn told her. 'I can't give him the life I want him to have but she can. If William hadn't died it would have been different but he isn't so I've got to do what's best for our son.'

A sob escaped as she said this and she wiped some tears away.

'It's going to take a few days for Gwyneth to get here so I'll have the first few days with him. It's not like I won't see him again or know what he's doing.'

'What are you doing about registering his birth?' Betty asked her.

'I'm going to wait until Gwyneth and Bert are here and then they can register him in their names. Gwyneth has been staying away from home looking after an aunt of ours for a couple of months, so when she turns up back home with a baby, it will be a surprise but no-one will question it. She'll just say she didn't know until the last minute. He'll be their baby, I'll just be his aunt.'

'It sounds like it could work but it's going to be hard on you,' Betty said.

'It's the best thing to do for my son,' Wyn replied,' so I'm fine about it.'

Betty knew when to shut up so didn't reply.

CHAPTER TWENTY THREE

The next day Betty was getting ready to leave. Wyn walked over to her, put her arms around her, 'I'm really happy you were here to see him born.' she told her.

'I'm happy I was here too,' Betty replied. 'What are you going to call him? You can't just keep calling him, the baby or him.'

'I'm letting Gwyneth choose the name as he is going to be her son,' Wyn told her.

'How long before they get here?' Betty asked.

'Martha sent the telegraph to her this morning so she and Bert should be here in a couple of days.'

The doorbell rang at that moment, 'that'll be Ned,' Betty said. She looked at Wyn with tears in her eyes, 'are you sure you're going to be alright?' she asked.

'Yes I will be,' Wyn replied. 'It'll be better once the baby has gone and I start working in the shop.'

Betty kissed her and told her she would see her soon.

'Maybe I'll come and see you,' Wyn replied, 'it would be nice to see everyone again.'

They kissed again and Betty walked down the steps to the car where Ned was waiting. She waved as she got in and Ned drove off.

Wyn walked back into the house sadly and went up to where the baby was sleeping in his basket. She looked down at him and gently stroked his face. She could see a slight resemblance to William in his face.

'Your father would have loved you,' she told him, 'but your new mum and dad will love you just as much and you'll have a good life with them. I'll always be around to help you if you ever need me.'

She wiped away the tears that had started streaming down her face and stood up straight as she heard Martha coming back into the house. She left the room to meet her.

'I've got a telegraph for you,' Martha told her.

She put it into Wyn's outstretched hand.

'It's a reply from Gwyneth,' Wyn told her. 'They'll be here tomorrow.'

Martha sighed and shook her head.

'I hope this is what you really want,' she commented.

'We'd have managed.'

'I don't want to just manage,' Wyn replied. 'I want more than that for my son.'

'I know said,' Martha, 'it's just very sad that's all.'

She patted Wyn's hand and walked out of the door.

Wyn looked down at her son, 'we'd better get your stuff packed,' she told him, 'you're going home tomorrow.'

It was early the next day when a carriage arrived outside the house. Wyn had been watching for it and opened the front door before they had a chance to ring the bell.

Gwyneth walked straight up to her and took her into her arms. Wyn sighed and pulled her close.

'Are you alright?' Gwyneth asked her.

'I'm not bad,' Wyn replied, 'I'll be glad to get this over with. You're looking very well though. You were always very pretty and you look exactly the same.'

'She certainly does,' said a voice behind Wyn.

'Oh Wyn, I don't know if you remember Bert, we used to meet him up the hill when we were kids but he left when his granddad died. He came back a few years ago, we bumped into each other in the High Street one day and recognised each other straight away. One thing led to another and we ended up married.'

'Yes of course I remember, his grandfather used to tell us lots of stories. I didn't realise it was him you married,' she turned to Bert, 'it's nice to see you again,' she told him.

'Come in and meet your new son.' Wyn showed them up to the bedroom where the baby was lying in his basket. Gwyneth looked down at him, 'he's lovely,' she said, 'can I pick him up?'

'Of course you can, he's your son,' replied Wyn. Gwyneth picked him up and Wyn could see it was love at first sight. Bert walked over to Gwyneth and took the baby off her. Wyn could tell he was also full of emotion.

'We'll take good care of him,' they both told her. 'We'll do our best for him.'

'I know,' Wyn replied, 'that's why I want him to live with you.'

Martha brought them up a pot of tea and as they were drinking, Gwyneth brought Wyn up to date about their family and friends in Penarth. Her other sister Elizabeth was also married and had four children, and her brother Robert was away in the army. Wyn told her the last news she had heard about Henry as he had never been heard of again by his family. Her parents had both died without ever knowing what had happened to their eldest son.

'Not that father ever wanted to know,' added Gwyneth, 'but mother would have liked to know even though he was only her step son.'

Bert hadn't joined in the conversation, he was just staring down into the face of his new son. It made Wyn very sad to watch as it made her think about how it would have been

with William and how proud he would have been of his son, but she was comforted knowing how much they already loved him. Martha came back into the room and asked Gwyneth and Bert how long they were staying in London.
'We thought we might stay tonight and get the train back to Wales tomorrow morning,' they told her.
'Would you like to stay here?' she asked.
Gwyneth looked at Wyn, 'please do stay,' Wyn pleaded.
'You can sleep in my room with the baby, I'll sleep in the small bedroom down the hall.'
Gwyneth looked at Bert who nodded. 'That'll be very kind of you,' she told them, 'we'd love to stay here.'
'The Registry Office is still open,' Wyn told them, 'you could register his birth today, it'll get it out of the way.'
'That's a good idea,' Bert agreed, 'we'll be able to get away earlier tomorrow.'
Wyn cleared the huge lump that had formed in her throat and asked Gwyneth, what they were going to call him.
'We thought Edwin after Bert's granddad and William after his own father.'
'Thank you,' whispered Wyn, 'his dad would have liked that. Edwin William Hook is a good name.'
When they had finished their tea Gwyneth and Bert took Edwin to have him registered as their son.
The next morning they were ready to leave quite early. Wyn had found it strange to be sleeping in a different room to her son, especially when she could hear him crying. She had been very uncomfortable when her breasts had filled with milk and she hadn't fed him. He had already been introduced to his new milk in a bottle and was taking to it

very well. She knew her milk would dry up soon but at the moment it didn't feel right not to be feeding him.

'How was it last night?' she asked Gwyneth.

'I loved sitting in the rocking chair feeding him,' Gwyneth replied, 'I didn't think it would be so wonderful.'

Wyn gave a small smile and said 'I'm glad, I want all of you to be happy.'

'We will,' said Bert coming up behind her. He turned to Gwyneth, 'the carriage is here, it's time to go if we're going to get the train,'

Bert took the bags and moses basket out to the carriage and then came back to get Gwyneth and Edwin. Wyn hugged Gwyneth hard, kissed Edwin on the head and ran back into the house crying.

'Don't worry,' Martha told them, 'she'll be alright, I'll look after her.

Gwyneth climbed into the carriage, Bert handed her Edwin and then climbed in himself. They could see Wyn standing at the window and they both waved as the carriage moved off. Wyn watched until they had disappeared then turned back into the room. She fell into Martha's waiting arms and sobbed her heart out for a long time.

CHAPTER TWENTY FOUR

Over the next few days the discomfort in Wyn's breasts started to subside and they stopped leaking milk. The pain of losing her baby was still as strong but she knew they had arrived back in Wales and Bob, as he had already become known, was happy and healthy as Gwyneth had written to her. She had started working in the confectionary shop for Tommy and was really enjoying it. She loved the time of day when all the kids would leave school and rush into the shop to choose what sweets they wanted. Sometimes it took them a long time to pick from all the jars on the shelves but she never got impatient and rushed them. All the mothers liked her because she was so patient with their children. There was one child in particular that she developed a soft spot for. His name was Martin and he had a mop of ginger curly hair and a mass of freckles on his face. He was a cheeky, mischievous child who was always getting into trouble but Wyn couldn't help liking him. The things he did were naughty but never hurt anyone. He never had any money but still came into the shop. He would stand at the counter and look up at her with his big eyes and a cheeky grin on his face. Wyn couldn't resist. She would just have to give him a bag of sweets.

'He takes advantage of you,' Tommy told her but he didn't try to stop her doing it.

One day she heard shouting coming from outside the shop and went to investigate. She saw Martin sitting on the roof of a shed in the garden of the house opposite waiting for people to pass by then throwing jumping jacks onto the road after they had walked by making them jump. A crowd had gathered and they were all shouting at him. Martin was

refusing to come down and was just sitting there poking his tongue out at them. Wyn smiled wryly to herself and thought, that boy, he's going to push people too far one day. She walked over the road and looked up at Martin.
'Come down and say you're sorry' she told him.
'Why should I?' he replied. 'I wasn't doing nothing.'
'That's not how it looked from where I was,' Wyn told him. 'I saw what you were doing, Now come down otherwise you're going to be in big trouble.'
Martin looked at her and smiled sweetly. 'Can I have some sweets if I do?' he asked.
'Say you're sorry and mean it,' Wyn answered.
'I'm sorry,' Martin said in a small voice.
Wyn could see he didn't mean it but everyone had started leaving so she didn't say anymore. She felt sorry for him because of the way he had to live. He was quite often hungry and always looked grubby but, although his clothes were threadbare, they were always clean. His parents lived in a very rough area and tried their best but having nine children made things tough for all of them. Wyn always gave the children sweets when she saw them and would love to have been able to help them more but knew there wasn't much she could do. Tommy couldn't understand why she could felt so sorry for them although he suspected she was thinking about her own son so he didn't say anything.
One day Martin came running into the shop.
'You'll never guess what,' he said excitedly.
'I can't guess so you'll have to tell me,' Wyn answered with a smile.

'We're going on holiday,' Martin told her. 'We're going hopping in Kent.'

He seemed to be so excited Wyn couldn't bring herself to tell him that hopping wasn't really a holiday but was very hard work.

'When are you going?' Wyn asked.

'Tomorrow,' he replied.

Wyn felt sad that she wouldn't see him for a while but thought, maybe it'll be nicer in the country for him, it's not exactly fun for him here.

'Come into the shop with me,' she told him. She took some jars down from the shelf and filled several bags with sweets.

'Here take these,' she said. 'They will keep you all going during the journey.'

She was surprised and moved when Martin reached up and gave her a kiss.

'Thanks,' he said as he ran back towards his home. He stopped on the corner and waved to her. That was the last time she saw him. She found out later that his father had been given a farm hands job in Kent. She felt sad that she would never see Martin again but knew it would be a better life for all the family and Martin would be much happier down there. All the children were even going to school.

As the weeks passed Wyn found she was becoming quite happy and content. She still missed her son but liked what was happening in her life. Sometimes she found Tommy looking at her with a huge smile on his face. She knew he was becoming fond of her but didn't know how she felt about him. She still missed William and her baby but she liked Tommy and knew she had to get on with her life. Her baby weight had gone and she was back to her slim self. She had been saving money for a while as she wanted a new dress for Betty's wedding which was in three weeks' time. She and Betty were having dresses made for them and Wyn was going back to Mrs Brompton's house at the weekend, when Betty had her day off, to see the dressmaker and Wyn was really looking forward to it. She had been looking in the posh magazines they sold in the shop to see what kind of dress she might like but they were all too dressy for her. After all, it was a wedding not a posh ball, she thought to herself.

It was Saturday and Wyn was off to meet Betty after she had finished work. The shop closed at twelve on a Saturday so she would have plenty of time. She was just putting her hat on when Tommy came up behind her.

'You look very smart,' he told her taking her hand and putting a wad of pounds notes into it. Wyn looked up at him in shock.

'What's this for?' she asked.

'Just buy yourself a wonderful dress,' he said, 'if I'm escorting you to this wedding, you have to look nice for me.' this last bit was said with a smile.

Wyn gave him a big smile, kissed him on the cheek and said, 'Thank you, I'll choose something so nice you'll be happy to come with me.'

'I'd be happy if you wore a sack,' he said with a leer.

Wyn left the shop laughing.

When she got to the house Betty was waiting for her.

'The dressmaker is a bit late,' she told her, 'but come up to my room, we'll get ourselves ready for her. We have the house to ourselves for a while as Ned has driven Mrs

Brompton to have lunch at the Ritz with her future husband and Mrs Davis has gone to visit her sister.' Wyn followed Betty upstairs to her bedroom.

'This brings back memories,' she commented as they entered the room.

Betty turned and put her arm around her and pulled her close.

'I've missed this,' Betty said as she turned her face to kiss Wyn on the lips.

'Me too,' replied Wyn as she opened her mouth to deepen the kiss.

Betty moaned, 'we've got time if you want to,' she told her. Wyn didn't reply just moved her hands down to rub her finger over Betty's nipples. They fell onto the bed and nearly ripped each other's clothes off. Betty kissed her way down Wyn's body until she reached the heart of her sex. She moved her tongue round and round until Wyn arched her body and cried out in pleasure. Wyn pulled Betty back up the bed and kissed her hard on the lips. She could taste herself but didn't mind. She moved down and took a nipple in her mouth and sucked hard. Betty moaned, 'use your finger,' she whispered. Wyn moved her finger down and moved it round and round the nub of her sex going faster and faster at the same time sucking on her nipples. Betty gave a loud cry as the pleasure in her body rose to a peak. Afterwards they lay cuddled together in a satisfied silence.

'That'll probably be the last time we ever do that,' Betty told her, 'now that I'm going to be a married woman I've got to save myself for Ned.'

'I know,' replied Wyn smiling, 'I'm going to miss it though. I would never do that with any other woman but you.'

The doorbell suddenly rang and they jumped out of bed and pulled their clothes on quickly. Wyn sat back down on the bed as Betty ran down to the door to let the dressmaker in. Betty had already organised her wedding dress, so this was just for a dress for Wyn. She had decided to have a jacket and skirt made out of a light material. The jacket would be tight waisted and the skirt would be tight over the hips but then flowing to the hemline.

'You are going to look lovely,' Betty told her.

Wyn was to go back for a fitting the following week. Once the dressmaker had gone Wyn kissed Betty goodbye and made her way back to Martha's house.

The next day was Sunday and Martha had invited Tommy round for dinner. When he arrived he kissed Martha on the cheek and asked her where Wyn was.

'She's gone for a walk,' Martha told him. 'She's feeling very sad today and just wanted to be by herself.'

'I feel sad for her,' Tommy told her, 'she's such a lovely person.'

'You really like her don't you?'

'Yes I do,' Tommy replied, 'I intend to marry her one day.' Martha looked at him in surprise.

'Do you think she'll marry you?' she asked him.

'I hope so,' he replied, 'I know she likes me, I'll just have to work on her.'

Martha just smiled at him, 'I hope it happens, she deserves some happiness.'

When Wyn got back, he started telling her funny stories making her laugh out loud.
'Oh you have cheered me up,' she told him. 'I don't know what I'd do without you.'
Tommy looked at Martha who smiled back at him. The following day at work Tommy started flirting with her making her smile. Every time she walked past him he would touch her arm or stroke her face. At first, it made her jump but the more he did it, the more she found herself liking it. Oh my, she thought to herself, am I falling for him? The thought of it made her feel happy, which surprised her after all that had happened.
The day of Betty's wedding had arrived and Wyn was feeling quite excited. Things were happening between her and Tommy and she was very happy about it. I really like him she thought to herself. I think I could be very happy with him. She was hoping that after the wedding something would happen between them and she made sure she was wearing her best underclothes just in case. When she had done her hair and got dressed in her new clothes, she looked at herself in the mirror. Not bad she thought even if I do say so myself. As Tommy had given her the extra money she had been able to buy a jacket and skirt made of a better material. She loved the way the skirt fell and swirled at the ankle. She pinched her cheeks to put some colour in them, took one more look at herself and walked down the stairs. She was surprised to see Tommy waiting at the bottom smiling up at her.
'You're early,' she told him, 'we haven't even had breakfast yet.'

'I couldn't wait to see you,' he replied, 'you look beautiful.'
Wyn flushed with pleasure but didn't reply. They walked into the kitchen where Martha was just putting porridge into bowls.
'I didn't think you'd want much,' she said, 'so I've just made this.'
'You were right,' Wyn told her, 'I'm too excited to eat much,' although she did manage to finish a large bowl full. When it was time to leave Wyn skipped out of the door.
'Come on you two,' she said, 'hurry up, we don't want to be late.'
'Slow down,' they told her, 'we've got plenty of time.' Tommy grabbed hold of her hand and pushed it through his arm so she would walk slower. She looked up at him and smiled but didn't pull her hand away. Martha walked beside them smiling in pleasure at the sight of them. It looks like Tommy is going to get his wish she thought to herself.
When they arrived at the church, Wyn walked over to where Mrs Davis was standing. She gave her a big hug. Mrs Davis looked at her closely.
'You look very well,' she commented, 'how is everything?'
'I feel very well,' Wyn replied. 'I'm getting used to things now and Martha and Tommy are very kind to me.' She smiled at her as she said this.
'I'm glad,' Mrs Davis told her.
At that moment a very nervous looking Ned turned up. He didn't speak but gave them a smile as he walked into the church.
'I think we had better go in,' Mrs Davis told them.

They walked into the church and took a seat at the front. Wyn and Tommy were acting as witnesses. Betty had earlier asked Wyn to be her attendant, but her and Ned had changed their minds about a big wedding, so there was no attendant and no best man. The organ started playing as Betty entered the church and started walking down the aisle on the arm of an uncle Wyn had never met. There had been a lot of discussions about who would give Betty away as she didn't have much family left alive. She had only remembered this uncle at the last minute and was relieved when she found he was still alive and was happy to give her away. Wyn looked at her and smiled as she walked past. She looked beautiful in her wedding dress. Wyn had already seen it when she had gone for her last fitting as Betty was having hers at the same time. Mrs Brompton had given her the extremely expensive dress she had worn at her wedding to Mr Charles. Her daughter, Catherine hadn't wanted it for her wedding and it was just sitting in the attic. Betty had it altered to fit her and made a bit more up to date and it looked wonderful on her. Betty reached Ned's side and he turned to look at her. Wyn saw the way he smiled down at her, I want someone to look at me like that she thought.

After the ceremony, they all walked back to the house where there was a wedding breakfast waiting for them. Wyn walked over to Betty and gave her a big hug.

'Are you happy?' she asked her.

'Oh yes!' very replied Betty.

Wyn turned to Ned, 'look after her,' she told him, 'I hope you both will be very happy together.'

'We will,' Ned replied, 'I hope things work out better for you too.'

'I think they might,' Wyn replied him, looking over at Tommy.

'I see,' Ned said winking at her.

Wyn just smiled and walked back over to Tommy. All too soon it was time for Betty and Ned to leave for their honeymoon. They were going down to a guest house in Brighton. Betty had never been to the seaside before and was very excited. She looked very happy as she and Ned ran through a line of guests throwing rice over them and climbed into the motor car that Mrs Brompton had let them borrow. She threw her bouquet and Wyn caught it. Betty looked at Tommy and gave Wyn a knowing look, making her blush. Tommy just smiled.

When they had gone, Wyn said goodbye to Mrs Davis, then she, Tommy and Martha made their way home.

'Ooh that was wonderful,' Wyn sighed, 'they looked so happy.'

'It'll be your turn one day,' Martha told her.

'I hope so,' Wyn replied wistfully.

When they got home Martha tactfully left them alone.

'Did you enjoy yourself?' Wyn asked Tommy.

'It was a wonderful day,' he replied. 'They looked very happy together.'

He pulled her towards him, put his hand under her chin and tipped her mouth up to his. He kissed her gently at first but suddenly moaned and started kissing her passionately.

Wyn pulled away from him, 'we can't, not here,' she told him.'

He gave a huge sigh, 'you're right, come into the shop tomorrow, we can be alone there.'
'What would I tell Martha?' she asked.
'Tell her we're stocktaking,' he replied.
He gave her another kiss then reluctantly opened the front door.
'I'll see you tomorrow then?' he asked.
Wyn just nodded and shut the door. She walked slowly up the stairs. Martha opened her bedroom door.
'Has he gone already?' she asked.
'Yes,' he suddenly remembered we have to stock take tomorrow so he went back to get the books ready,' Wyn told her.
'I don't know,' Martha said, 'all that man thinks about is work, is he making you go in as well?'
'Yes, but I don't mind,' Wyn replied.
Wyn went into her bedroom but just sat on the bed thinking. She stood up, stripped her clothes off and looked at her naked body in the mirror. Not too bad considering I've had a baby she thought, running her hands over her body. She shivered with anticipation as she thought of Tommy's hands touching her. I can't wait she thought.
The following day she was at the shop bright and early, full of excited anticipation. As soon as she walked in the door Tommy pulled her towards him and kissed her passionately.
'I've been awake most of the night thinking about this moment,' he told her.
She could feel his large erection pushing against her and the passion started rising in her. 'Come upstairs,' he said, 'I want to feel your naked body against me.'

Wyn followed him up the stairs and into his bedroom. Tommy started kissing her again and they fell onto the bed clawing at each other's clothes, impatient for them both to be naked. Tommy entered her straight away, unable to wait any longer. Wyn didn't mind, she felt the same way. He started moving slowly and Wyn could feel the pleasure building in her.

'Faster!' she said, 'oh go faster.' She felt the passion rising and knew it wasn't going to take long. She could hear Tommy moaning out loud.

'Oh Wyn,' he was saying, 'I love you so.'

The intense pleasure she was feeling made Wyn's back arch and then cry out as she came. She felt Tommy suddenly still and then he shouted out loud with pleasure as his seed spilled into her. Afterwards they lay together contentedly.

'Did you mean what you said,? Wyn asked him, 'you know, when you said you loved me.' 'Oh yes,' he replied, 'I love you very much.'

He suddenly slipped off the bed and onto his knees in front of her. He took her hand in his. Wyn sat up down at him. 'Marry me, Wyn please,' he asked, 'we could be so happy together.'

With tears in her eyes, Wyn replied, 'yes, yes, yes, I'd love to marry you. I love you too. I never thought I would love anyone else but I really do.'

Tommy just kissed her hard on the mouth and hugged her tight. Wyn could feel him shaking and knew he was full of emotion. After a while he let her go, 'let it be soon,' he said, 'I can't wait.'

EPILOGUE

Wyn and Tommy got married a couple of months later and spent many happy years together. Aunt Wyn died in 1963 aged 83. My grandfather didn't know she was his mother until he read her diaries, found after her death. It came as a great shock to him. Wyn never returned to Wales to live although she did visit Gwyneth and Bob a few times. She didn't have any more children, which was a shame as she would always have a kiss and a cuddle with all of the children in the family. She used to keep a supply of humbugs in her pocket and would hand them out to whatever child came near her. I wasn't very old when she died but my memory of her was of a very kind lady who spoke very quietly and smelt of lavender.

Why she didn't ever tell her son no-one could understand, although to have an illegitimate child in 1900 was a bit different to these days. It's a normal thing now but back then she would have been ostracised and Bob's life would have been miserable. Although his life was a happy one, he hated going down the mine and ran away at least twice to try to join the army, but his life is another story.

Made in the USA
Charleston, SC
25 May 2016